AMERICA BOWL

44 PRESIDENTS ★VS★ 44 SUPER BOWLS

by
Don Steinberg

Rb
Flash
Point

ROARING BROOK PRESS ★ NEW YORK

Published by Flash Point, an imprint of Roaring Brook Press
Roaring Brook Press is a division of Holtzbrinck Publishing Holdings Limited Partnership
175 Fifth Avenue, New York, New York 10010

Distributed in Canada by H. B. Fenn and Company Ltd.

Library of Congress Cataloging-in-Publication Data

Steinberg, Don, 1962–
   America Bowl : 44 U.S. presidents vs. 44 Super Bowls / Don Steinberg. — 1st ed.
     p. cm.
   ISBN 978-1-59643-683-1
   1. Presidents—United States—History—Miscellanea—Juvenile literature. 2. United States—Politics and government—Miscellanea—Juvenile literature. 3. Super Bowl—History—Miscellanea—Juvenile literature. I. Title.

E176.1.S717 2010
973.09′9,—dc22

2010027708

Roaring Brook Press books are available for special promotions and premiums.
For details contact: Director of Special Markets, Holtzbrinck Publishers.

First Edition November 2010
Printed in October 2010 in the United States of America by RR Donnelley & Sons Company, Harrisonburg, Virginia
10 9 8 7 6 5 4 3 2 1

INTRODUCTION

I *was eight years old when my mother bought me a set of little plastic statues of America's presidents.*

They were about three inches tall, all in slightly different poses. Thomas Jefferson, the third president, was immortalized with his left arm extended. Harry Truman, the thirty-third president, had both of his hands out in front of him, like he was trying to stop a crowd rushing toward him. Franklin Delano Roosevelt, who was confined to a wheelchair as president but hid it from the public, was standing straight and tall like all the other guys, with a fancy black cape hanging over his left shoulder. William Howard Taft and Grover Cleveland and William McKinley were molded as big, barrel-chested men.

All of this was important because I was, you know, a kid, and the presidents became part of my toy collection. And I did with them what any creative, overstimulated kid did with toys—I made them talk to each other, and play football and hockey against each other, and, uh, fight each other. I have to tell you, Jefferson's extended arm served him well when it came time to rumble—it worked like a pesky left jab.

The heavy guys didn't always win. Sometimes I'd take McKinley or Cleveland in one hand and a skinny president like Abraham Lincoln or Woodrow Wilson in the other. I'd slide them toward each other on a smooth floor or a table and let go, and when they collided in the middle it wasn't always the skinny one that went down. Sometimes a thin president like Calvin Coolidge or John F. Kennedy would be standing there, looking down on his bigger, fallen opponent. It was my first exposure to rough-and-tumble politics, I guess.

My mom was a little disturbed that I was using the presidents as fighting action figures. And she didn't even see some of the other stuff I did (I believe I once got a Super Ball and used the presidents as bowling pins). But the statues accomplished their purpose. They taught me a little bit about history. When I was done playing with them, I'd put all the presidents back on a special stand, arranged by number. Of course I memorized the order: Jackson 7, Van Buren 8, Harrison 9. It was the same way I was memorizing the facts on my baseball cards and football cards, and reading sports magazines. The Super Bowl was a pretty new thing back then. Its numbers were just my size, even though they were in roman numerals: VII, VIII, IX. I felt like I hadn't missed too much.

In college I studied political science. But what I really liked was sports. Eventually I became a

sports writer at a newspaper and started covering boxing, a sport where guys try to knock each other down. I had fulfilled my destiny.

On January 20, 2009, Barack Obama was sworn in as the forty-fourth president of the United States. I knew from my plastic statues that he wasn't the forty-fourth person to be president. Grover Cleveland was the twenty-second president and the twenty-fourth president. But Obama was number 44. Shortly into the Obama administration I realized something else. The next Super Bowl to be played, in January 2010, would be Super Bowl XLIV. Number 44! For one year only, the president and the Super Bowl would be the same number. And so, I figured, with the sides all even for one brief period of time—in all of history—there was only one thing to do. Unite all the presidents together on the same team and unleash them to battle once more.

And so here it is: America Bowl. Our presidents versus our Super Bowls to determine once and for all which have been "better." A contest of 44 individual matchups, one at a time. One point awarded per match. May the best American institution win.

We begin with George Washington, the father of our country, versus Super Bowl I, the mother of all Super Bowl games. The winner of that matchup gets one point for its side. It just gets better from there. By the end we'll have Barack Obama against Super Bowl XLIV, the comeback win by the New Orleans Saints over the Indianapolis Colts in 2010. In between, it's the most fun you can have learning about America's presidents and Super Bowls without having to read two separate books.

It's all in here. All the stars and all the goats. Joe Montana and Joe Namath. Watergate and "wide right." Tom Brady and Thomas Jefferson. "The Tackle" and the New Deal. Hey, what other book offers the scoop on Franklin Delano Roosevelt and William "the Refrigerator" Perry?

It turns out that 44 is a great number for this kind of completely bogus sporting event. It breaks easily into halves, and even into four quarters. And 44 points is a pretty typical score total for a real football game. If you want to experience this like a real game, don't skip ahead. Read one match at a time.

How did I decide which is "better" in each match—a Super Bowl or its same-number presi-

dent? Well, the main question is, How well did each president or Super Bowl achieve its purpose? I started with the idea that the best Super Bowl is equal to the best president, and worked down from there. Was the Super Bowl game truly super, or a letdown? Did the president accomplish much in office and leave a legacy, or become forgotten to everyone except those who didn't destroy their plastic statues on a Hot Wheels track or engulf them in modeling clay? In the end, it's a judgment call, of course. If you make up a game, you get to call the shots. So that's what I did.

To a lot of people it makes no sense to compare the presidents against the Super Bowls, to determine which have been "better." Yes, I've been called a lunatic, been advised to get a life. But to me, it seems crazy not to do this while we have the chance. Super Bowls and presidencies are the pinnacle of achievement in the United States. They're the biggest deals we have. They are America. So let the game begin.

HOME STATE: Virginia **PARTY:** Federalist

DATES AS PRESIDENT: 1789–1797

AGE AS PRESIDENT: 57 **REASON LEFT OFFICE:** Retired

ELECTORAL VOTES: 1789: Washington 69, Adams 34, Jay 9, others 15

1792: Washington 132, Adams 77, Clinton 50, others 11

GEORGE WASHINGTON

I am the father of our country!

Washington was the only president who didn't live in Washington, D.C. The nation's capital moved from New York to Phila-delphia in 1790 while the "Federal City" (Washington, D.C.) was being built.

The opening matchup of America Bowl is a meeting of **bold new ideas.**

It pits the first Super Bowl—Packers vs. Chiefs—against the first U.S. president, George Washington. Each was unforgettable in its, or his, own way, blazing a trail for those that would come later.

Like the creation of the United States, the first AFL–NFL championship game was the result of a long, fierce battle (between the leagues), then months of negotiation. The Kansas City Chiefs came with talent and flair, but few expected them to challenge the NFL dynasty Green Bay Packers. The Chiefs did run with Vince Lombardi's Pack in the first half, but Green Bay pulled away in the second half with three unanswered touchdowns (TDs), including two short bursts into the end zone by running back (RB) Elijah Pitts and a sweet Max McGee grab of a Bart Starr pass. Adding injury to the insult, in the fourth quarter boastful Chiefs defensive back (DB) Fred "the Hammer" Williamson was knocked out cold when his head hit Packers RB Donny Anderson's knee—eliciting smirks from Packers veterans on the sidelines.

The game was historic . . . but not much of a surprise.

Everyone in America who voted for president, in both 1789 and 1792, voted for George Washington—a record he still holds. Everything Washington did as president was new, and nobody knew how things were going to turn out. At first they didn't even know if America should have a president—back in England they had kings. John Adams suggested that even if he was president, people should call Washington "your highness." But George settled for "father of our

Green Bay Packers
QB Bart Starr

The National Football League (NFL) was formed in 1920. The American Football League (AFL) started in 1960. They started competing for the best players and developed a bitter rivalry. For several years before they formally merged together in 1970, the leagues agreed to have their respective champions play each other at the end of the season.

country." Inaugural address? Washington's second one was the shortest in history—less than two minutes. In eight years in office, he defined what it meant to be president. He led the army, delegated jobs wisely, held our fragile new nation together, and proved to countries around the world that the American experiment would stand. After two terms he retired, and presidents for more than a century afterward kept to that limit even though it wasn't required by law (yet). The rest, as they say, is history homework. **Score Game One for the Presidents!**

SUPER BOWL I

SCORE: Green Bay Packers 35, Kansas City Chiefs 10 **DATE:** January 15, 1967
LOCATION: Los Angeles Memorial Coliseum, Los Angeles, CA
REGULAR SEASON RECORDS: Packers 14–2, Chiefs 12–2–1
GAME MVP: Packers QB Bart Starr **TV AUDIENCE:** 51.18 million
COST OF 30-SECOND COMMERCIAL: $42,000

★ *Score After this Match* ★

PRESIDENTS	1
SUPER BOWLS	0
QUARTER	○ ● ● ●

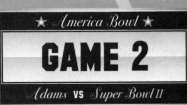

HOME STATE: Massachusetts **PARTY:** Federalist
DATES AS PRESIDENT: 1797–1801
AGE AS PRESIDENT: 61 **REASON LEFT OFFICE:** lost re-election
ELECTORAL VOTES: 1796: Adams 71, Jefferson 68, Pinckney 59, Burr 30, others 48
1800: Jefferson 73, Burr 73, Adams 65, Pinckney 64, Jay 1

Adams barely won—he beat Jefferson by three electoral votes.

JOHN ADAMS

Super Bowl II *wasn't even technically called a* **Super Bowl** *yet.*

The game barely deserved it. It wasn't super. The NFL champion Packers were favored by 14 points, and won by 19, over the AFL's Oakland Raiders. The Oakland defense, not-very-famously nicknamed "Eleven Angry Men," held game MVP Bart Starr to one passing touchdown, but Packers kicker Don Chandler nailed four field goals (FGs) and Green Bay DB Herb Adderly picked off a pass from Raiders quarter back (QB) Daryle Lamonica and took it back 60 yards for a defensive TD. The Raiders probably were angrier men after the game. The big story was that legendary Packers coach Vince Lombardi might retire after the game, seemingly with nothing left to prove. And he did. At halftime, Packers guard Jerry Kramer announced to his teammates, "Let's play the last 30 minutes for the old man." He wasn't talking about John Adams.

Adams had a lot to prove as president. Before winning the big job, he'd been legitimately super. He pulled the strings behind the American Revolution. He pretty much got Thomas Jefferson to write the Declaration of Independence. He engineered George Washington into the job as first president and, after working as Washington's VP, he got the job himself.

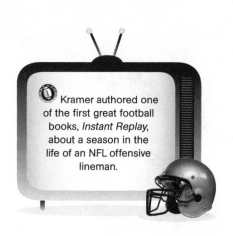

Kramer authored one of the first great football books, *Instant Replay*, about a season in the life of an NFL offensive lineman.

Oakland QB Daryle Lamonica actually did better than me, throwing for two TDs, both to Raiders receiver Bill Miller.

Green Bay Packers QB Bart Starr

But in office he had issues. Adams was caught between fellow Federalists like Alexander Hamilton, who wanted a strong national government, and Democratic-Republicans like Jefferson, who wanted more power for the people and feared that too much centralized power would mean the United States would be just like England bossing everyone around. Adams seemed to lean toward not really trusting the people. When criticism of the young U.S. government started to rise, he signed the awful Alien and Sedition Acts, making it a criminal act to write bad things about the government. Boo! His one term in office sometimes is called "miserable." But before leaving office he did pull a nifty move to avoid a war with France, and he started the U.S. Navy.

In the end, you have to give Adams credit for keeping it interesting. It's certainly more than you can say about Super Bowl II. **Score this for the Presidents.**

SUPER BOWL II

SCORE: Green Bay Packers 33, Oakland Raiders 14 **DATE:** January 14, 1968
LOCATION: Orange Bowl, Miami, FL
REGULAR SEASON RECORDS: Packers 9–4–1, Raidersm 13–1
GAME MVP: Packers QB Bart Starr **TV AUDIENCE:** 39.12 million
COST OF 30-SECOND COMMERCIAL: $54,000

★ *Score After this Match* ★

PRESIDENTS	2
SUPER BOWLS	0
QUARTER	○ ● ● ●

HOME STATE: Virginia
PARTY: Democratic-Republican
DATES AS PRESIDENT: 1801–1809
AGE AS PRESIDENT: 57
REASON LEFT OFFICE: Retired
ELECTORAL VOTES: 1800: Jefferson 73, Burr 73, Adams 65, Pinckney 64, Jay 1
1804: Jefferson 162, Pinckney 14

THOMAS JEFFERSON

Thomas Jefferson wrote the **Declaration of Independence.**

The third president defined American values and encoded them in a government built to maintain individual liberty. It's a resilient and glorious system that has endured more than two centuries.

But he didn't guarantee a victory.

That's what Jets QB "Broadway" Joe Namath did when he led the AFL champions into Super Bowl III against the NFL's mighty Baltimore Colts. It was one of the great upsets in American sports history.

It was the first truly super Super Bowl. Namath passed for 206 yards. Jets RB Matt Snell ran for 121 yards and a touchdown. The Colts didn't even score until the fourth quarter.

When the Jets did the impossible, dominating the Colts on both sides of the ball in a 16–7 win, it didn't just alter the balance of power in professional football, showing that the upstart AFL could compete with the established NFL. It

Jefferson believed that Washington and Adams had acted a bit too much like British kings. And yet, most notably, Jefferson doubled the size of America with the Louisiana Purchase.

8

ushered in a new era in sports. Jefferson himself said, "I hold it that a little rebellion now and then is a good thing, as necessary in the political world as storms in the physical." And now that Jeffersonian ideal was coming true on the gridiron. *Sports Illustrated* called it "the Age of Audacity"—a time of upheaval when outspoken athletes like Namath, Muhammad Ali, Jim Brown, and Bill Russell spoke out, and the Hendrix version of "All Along the Watchtower" was playing in the background.

This is an epic Presidents-vs.-Super Bowls matchup. Choosing a winner isn't, you know, self-evident. In the end, it comes down to who wants it more. Sorry, Joe. You have some serious style. But how can we go against TJ?

Score this for the Presidents.

WE GOT THIS!

Jets QB
Joe Namath

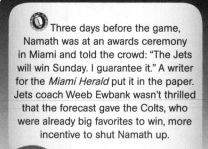

Three days before the game, Namath was at an awards ceremony in Miami and told the crowd: "The Jets will win Sunday. I guarantee it." A writer for the *Miami Herald* put it in the paper. Jets coach Weeb Ewbank wasn't thrilled that the forecast gave the Colts, who were already big favorites to win, more incentive to shut Namath up.

SUPER BOWL III

SCORE: New York Jets 16, Baltimore Colts 7 **DATE:** January 12, 1969
LOCATION: Orange Bowl, Miami, FL
REGULAR SEASON RECORDS: Jets 11–3, Colts 13–1
GAME MVP: Jets QB Joe Namath **TV AUDIENCE:** 41.66 million
COST OF 30-SECOND COMMERCIAL: $55,000

★ *Score After this Match* ★

PRESIDENTS	3
SUPER BOWLS	0
QUARTER	○ ● ● ●

HOME STATE: Virginia **PARTY:** Democratic-Republican
DATES AS PRESIDENT: 1809–1817
AGE AS PRESIDENT: 57 **REASON LEFT OFFICE:** Retired
ELECTORAL VOTES: 1808: Madison 122, Pinckney 47
1812: Madison 128, Clinton 89

JAMES MADISON

DID YOU KNOW that James Madison is the country's shortest president EVER? **He was only 5'4"!**

Yes, James Madison co-wrote the **Federalist Papers.**

He was a Founding Father. You can't take that away from him. But in the big chair, as president, well, we've had better. Madison's trade policies were questionable. He was outplayed by Napoleon and by the British, who took American seamen, hijacked maritime cargoes, and, after a declaration of war in 1812, entered Washington and set fire to the White House and the Capitol. Way to go.

Super Bowl IV, played in January 1970, wasn't an all-time classic, but at least no national institutions were torched. It was in New Orleans. Jazz trumpet guy Al Hirt played the national anthem, probably unaware that it had been composed in 1814 during Madison's presidency.

The Minnesota Vikings, led by coach Bud Grant, were favored to

Sadly, two of my vice presidents died while I was in office.

win. (Later, in 1970, Lou Grant, played by Ed Asner, was a popular Minneapolis-based TV character on the *Mary Tyler Moore Show*.) But the scrappy KC Chiefs scored an upset. They dominated from the start, winning 23–7. The Vikings didn't even score in the first half and had just 67 yards rushing. No rusher in the game ran for more than 39 yards. Chiefs wide receiver (WR) Otis Taylor had a 46-yard TD catch, and Len Dawson passed for 142 in all. The game's real star was the Chiefs' truly Ed Asner–like coach Hank Stram, who wore a microphone and rattled off hilarious sideline chatter like, "Just keep matriculating the ball down the field, boys."

Not a super-dee-duper Super Bowl, **but this one scorches Madison for the victory.**

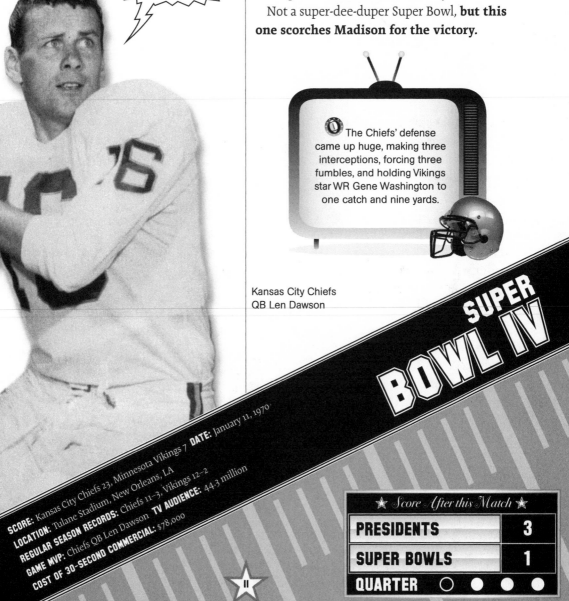

GO LONG!!!

The Chiefs' defense came up huge, making three interceptions, forcing three fumbles, and holding Vikings star WR Gene Washington to one catch and nine yards.

Kansas City Chiefs
QB Len Dawson

SUPER BOWL IV

SCORE: Kansas City Chiefs 23, Minnesota Vikings 7 **DATE:** January 11, 1970
LOCATION: Tulane Stadium, New Orleans, LA
REGULAR SEASON RECORDS: Chiefs 11–3, Vikings 12–2
GAME MVP: Chiefs QB Len Dawson **TV AUDIENCE:** 44.3 million
COST OF 30-SECOND COMMERCIAL: $78,000

★ *Score After this Match* ★	
PRESIDENTS	3
SUPER BOWLS	1
QUARTER	○ ● ● ●

HOME STATE: Virginia **PARTY:** Democratic-Republican
DATES AS PRESIDENT: 1817–1825
AGE AS PRESIDENT: 58 **REASON LEFT OFFICE:** Retired
ELECTORAL VOTES: 1816: Monroe 183, King 34
1820: Monroe 231, J.Q. Adams 1

JAMES **MONROE**

> Monroe was the third president in a row from Virginia, giving the state 24 straight years filling the White House.

Wait a minute—*is that the Baltimore Colts representing the American Football Conference?*

Yessiree. In this first official post-merger season, the Colts, Browns, and Steelers slid over from the NFL to the new AFC, as the unified league was split into two conferences and six divisions. That allowed two old-school NFL teams, the Colts and Cowboys, to play each other in Super Bowl V in Miami.

It was an exciting game, if you go by the final five seconds, when rookie Colts kicker Jim O'Brien nailed a 32-yard field goal to win it 16–13. The Colts had trailed 13–6 at the half, so it was an admirable comeback. But the game had so many messed-up plays, critics called it the "Blunder Bowl." There were 11 turnovers. Colts defensive end (DE) Bubba Smith supposedly refused

> I won the electoral votes of all but three states in 1816 and won every state in 1820.

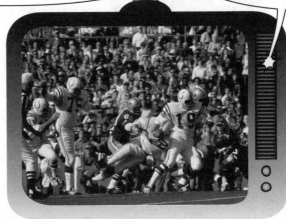

Two frustrating Colts drives in the fourth quarter ended in an end-zone interception by Cowboys linebacker (LB) Chuck Howley and a fumble into the end zone by Colts WR Ed Hinton.

The Colts tied the score at 13 only after intercepting a Cowboys pass and returning it to the Cowboys' three-yard line.

to wear his Super Bowl ring because the game was such a disaster.

Against such a clunker, you'd think James Monroe would cruise easily to victory. Not so fast! Yes, he's James Monroe of the Monroe Doctrine, the famous "get off my cloud" warning to other nations to keep their paws away from our side of the globe. Not many people leave doctrines as legacies. But we hear The Doc was actually written by John Quincy Adams. (JQA was so upset that Monroe took the credit, he supposedly refused to wear his Monroe Doctrine ring.)

So who wins? Despite not really authoring his own doctrine, Monroe helped keep the nation together and further define what America stood for. Against a Blunder Bowl? **We have to go with J-Roe.**

The Colts got some gratification after having lost the Super Bowl two years before to the Jets in the same stadium.

Baltimore Colts QB
Johnny Unitas

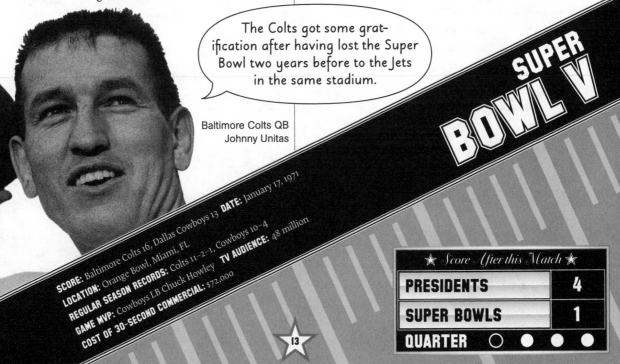

SUPER BOWL V

SCORE: Baltimore Colts 16, Dallas Cowboys 13 **DATE:** January 17, 1971
LOCATION: Orange Bowl, Miami, FL
REGULAR SEASON RECORDS: Colts 11–2–1, Cowboys 10–4
GAME MVP: Cowboys LB Chuck Howley **TV AUDIENCE:** 48 million
COST OF 30-SECOND COMMERCIAL: $72,000

★ *Score After this Match* ★

PRESIDENTS	4
SUPER BOWLS	1
QUARTER	○ ● ● ●

JOHN QUINCY ADAMS

HOME STATE: Massachusetts **PARTY:** Democratic-Republican
DATES AS PRESIDENT: 1825–1829
AGE AS PRESIDENT: 57 **REASON LEFT OFFICE:** Lost re-election
ELECTORAL VOTES: 1820: Monroe 231, J.Q. Adams 1 **1824:** J.Q. Adams 84, Jackson 99, Crawford 41, Clay 37 **1828:** Jackson 178, J.Q. Adams 83

> Did you know I was the second president (and the second Adams president) to serve only one term?

The Cowboys crushed Miami, 24–3, led by QB Roger Staubach and the Dallas **"Doomsday Defense."**

The game was in New Orleans, but they played outdoors and it was cold. It was 1972. We ordered 11 pizzas for this?

The Adamses were like the Mannings of presidents, the original family dynasty. Young

Adams passed the Tariff of 1828, fondly nicknamed the "Tariff of Abominations." It was a tax on items imported into the United States, which raised prices when people went shopping. That made people really mad.

Adams was a fine diplomat, but he became president under shady circumstances. There were five candidates in the election of 1824, and none received a majority of the electoral votes. So the decision went to the House of Representatives (thanks, Twelfth Amendment). Although Andrew Jackson had the most votes, the House of Representatives picked Adams. He would have needed to really stink up the place to lose against the lame Super Bowl VI.

Adams did have troubles with Congress. He admitted no new states to the union. He lost his re-election bid to Jackson. We ordered 11 pizzas for this? Still, that Super Bowl game was really terrible.

A close decision goes to Q—and the Presidents.

> This first Super Bowl win for the Cowboys was a huge deal in Texas.

> The Cowboys had lost a heartbreaker the year before and several crushing NFL Championhip games before that, including the famous 1967 "IceBowl" loss to Green Bay.

Dallas Cowboys QB Roger Staubach flips the ball to WRs Bob Hayes (left) and Lance Alworth

SUPER BOWL VI

SCORE: Dallas Cowboys 24, Miami Dolphins 3 **DATE:** January 16, 1972
LOCATION: Tulane Stadium, New Orleans, LA
REGULAR SEASON RECORDS: Cowboys 11–3, Dolphins 10–3–1
GAME MVP: Cowboys QB Roger Staubach **TV AUDIENCE:** 56.64 million
COST OF 30-SECOND COMMERCIAL: $86,000

★ Score After this Match ★	
PRESIDENTS	5
SUPER BOWLS	1
QUARTER	○ ● ● ●

HOME STATE: Tennessee **PARTY:** Democratic

DATES AS PRESIDENT: 1829–1837

AGE AS PRESIDENT: 61 **REASON LEFT OFFICE:** Retired

ELECTORAL VOTES: 1824: J.O. Adams 84, Jackson 99, Crawford 41, Clay 37

1824: Jackson 178, J.O. Adams 83 **1832:** Jackson 219, Clay 49

ANDREW JACKSON

What old-timers remember *about Super Bowl VII is a hilariously weasely pass near the end of the game, when Dolphins kicker Garo Yepremian picked up a blocked field goal, then thought he'd try throwing the ball.*

Harder than it looks! Garo blooped it into the hands of Redskins DB Mike Bass, who returned it all the way to the other end of the world for a touchdown. Other than that blooper, Miami's "No Name Defense" pitched a shutout. The Fins won 14–7 to wrap up their undefeated season. It made history, but the game itself wasn't particularly thrilling.

Jackson opened the White House to the public often. A huge mob attended his inauguration party, and once in 1837 he put a 1,400 pound block of cheese in the entrance hall for people to come and eat.

Andrew Jackson, a former commander of the Tennessee militia and military governor of Florida, brought a tough, frontier attitude to his two-term presidency. For much of his career, AJ had battled for turf against Indians—not football players with Indian pictures on their helmets, but real ones—and he was much more brutal than even the undefeated Miami Dolphins would ever be. To non-Indians, however, Jackson was a populist. He opposed the National Bank as an elite institution and fought for popular democracy. Old Hickory currently appears on one of the best stocking stuffers available, the $20 bill. **This victory goes to the presidency.**

The Dolphins went undefeated even though they lost their starting QB Bob Griese (broken leg) in week 5. Veteran 38-year-old QB Earl Morrall came off the bench and won the remaining games—as well as the NFL Comeback Player of the Year award.

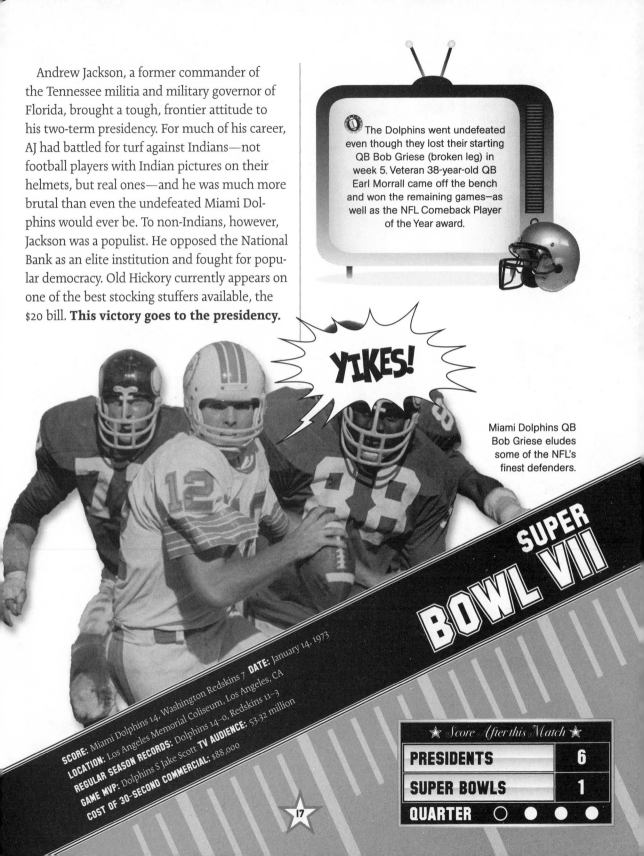

YIKES!

Miami Dolphins QB Bob Griese eludes some of the NFL's finest defenders.

SUPER BOWL VII

SCORE: Miami Dolphins 14, Washington Redskins 7 **DATE:** January 14, 1973
LOCATION: Los Angeles Memorial Coliseum, Los Angeles, CA
REGULAR SEASON RECORDS: Dolphins 14–0, Redskins 11–3
GAME MVP: Dolphins S Jake Scott **TV AUDIENCE:** 53.32 million
COST OF 30-SECOND COMMERCIAL: $88,000

★ *Score After this Match* ★

PRESIDENTS	6
SUPER BOWLS	1
QUARTER	○ ● ● ●

MARTIN VAN BUREN

HOME STATE: New York **PARTY:** Democratic
DATES AS PRESIDENT: 1837–1841
AGE AS PRESIDENT: 54 **REASON LEFT OFFICE:** Lost re-election
ELECTORAL VOTES: 1836: Van Buren 170, W.H. Harrison 73, White 26, Webster 14, Magnum 11
1840: W.H. Harrison 234, Van Buren 60 **1840:** Taylor 163, Class 127, Van Buren 0

Did you know *that the term* OK *is associated with Martin Van Buren, our eighth president?*

His nickname was Old Kinderhook. He was born in Kinderhook, N.Y. So that mostly explains that. Van Buren was a politician more than anything. He didn't want to upset anybody powerful. He appeased the Southern arm of the Democratic Party by coming out for free trade and saying

I had many nicknames, but my least favorite had to be "Martin Van Ruin."

he wouldn't abolish slavery. He wimped out in the Amistad case, sending a ship of captives to Cuba so as not to anger Spain. The economy tanked. He served just one term. But he did avoid another war with Great Britain and instituted some sound financial policies. And he pretty much started the Democratic Party. So he did . . . well, OK.

Super Bowl VIII may have been an even bigger letdown than Van Buren. The Dolphins were favored to win. They scored on the opening kickoff, and it was never close. They were up 17–zip at halftime and won 24–7. There wasn't a single passing touchdown in the game. Dolphins QB Bob Griese completed six passes total for 73 yards. The MVP was run-up-the-gut fullback (FB) Larry Csonka, who ran for 145 yards and two touchdowns. The halftime show featured Miss Texas 1973 playing a fiddle tribute to American music, titled "A Musical America." Make it stop! By the end, fans must have been begging for Van Buren. MVB! MVB! MVB for MVP!

It's another incredible dud of a game. **And the Presidents build their early lead on the scoreboard.**

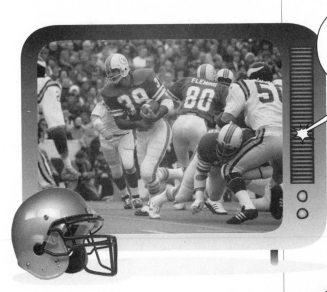

Did you know this was the first Super Bowl in which an original AFL team was the favorite?

SUPER BOWL VIII

SCORE: Miami Dolphins 24, Minnesota Vikings 7 **DATE:** January 13, 1974
LOCATION: Rice Stadium, Houston, TX
REGULAR SEASON RECORDS: Dolphins 12–2, Vikings 12–2
GAME MVP: Dolphins RB Larry Csonka **TV AUDIENCE:** 51.7 million
COST OF 30-SECOND COMMERCIAL: $103,000

★ Score After this Match ★	
PRESIDENTS	7
SUPER BOWLS	1
QUARTER	○ ● ● ●

HOME STATE: Virginia **PARTY:** Democratic
DATES AS PRESIDENT: 1841
AGE AS PRESIDENT: 68 **REASON LEFT OFFICE:** died in office
ELECTORAL VOTES: 1840: W.H. Harrison 234, Van Buren 60

WILLIAM HENRY HARRISON

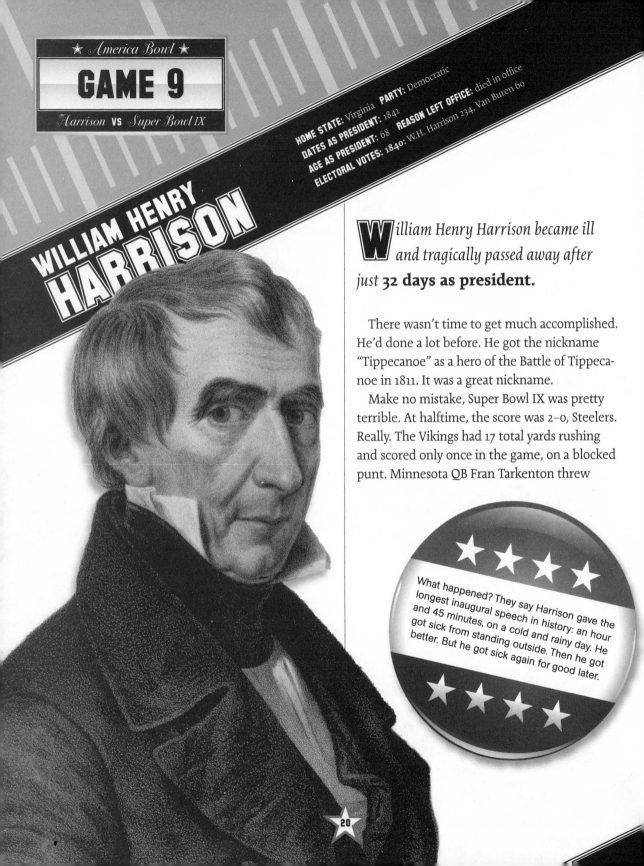

William Henry Harrison became ill and tragically passed away after just **32 days as president.**

There wasn't time to get much accomplished. He'd done a lot before. He got the nickname "Tippecanoe" as a hero of the Battle of Tippecanoe in 1811. It was a great nickname.

Make no mistake, Super Bowl IX was pretty terrible. At halftime, the score was 2–0, Steelers. Really. The Vikings had 17 total yards rushing and scored only once in the game, on a blocked punt. Minnesota QB Fran Tarkenton threw

What happened? They say Harrison gave the longest inaugural speech in history: an hour and 45 minutes, on a cold and rainy day. He got sick from standing outside. Then he got better. But he got sick again for good later.

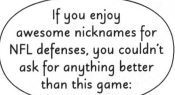

If you enjoy awesome nicknames for NFL defenses, you couldn't ask for anything better than this game:

The Steel Curtain vs. The Purple People Eaters.

three interceptions. But, how to put this: at least they played the whole thing.

Score one grim little point for the big game.

Pittsburgh Steelers
RB Franco Harris

SUPER BOWL IX

SCORE: Pittsburgh Steelers 16, Minnesota Vikings 6 **DATE:** January 12, 1975
LOCATION: Tulane Stadium, New Orleans, LA
REGULAR SEASON RECORDS: Steelers 10-3-1, Vikings 10-4
GAME MVP: Steelers RB Franco Harris **TV AUDIENCE:** 56 million
COST OF 30-SECOND COMMERCIAL: $107,000

★ Score After this Match ★	
PRESIDENTS	7
SUPER BOWLS	2
QUARTER	○ ● ● ●

21

HOME STATE: Virginia **PARTY:** Whig
DATES AS PRESIDENT: 1841–1845 **REASON LEFT OFFICE:** Retired
AGE AS PRESIDENT: 51
ELECTORAL VOTES: None

JOHN TYLER

John Tyler served nearly a complete term in office as president of the United States, despite **never being elected** to the office.

Tyler was vice president when William Henry Harrison passed away almost instantly after being inaugurated. Tyler stepped in as president and served without a VP, which was the deal back then. He did all right, though not good enough

Tyler was the first vice president to slide in as president due to a presidential death. Harrison had been elected using the campaign slogan "Tippecanoe and Tyler, too." Now America got to see who this "Tyler, too" guy was.

Lynn Swann was the first wide receiver to win a Super Bowl MVP award.

THAT'S RIGHT!

Pittsburgh Steelers
WR Lynn Swann

to get his picture on money. Tyler, at 51 the youngest president yet, was known for strengthening the presidency. The Virginian's greatest legacy probably is his annexation of Texas in 1845, an action that led to the Dallas Cowboys entering the NFL 115 years later.

Super Bowl X was a pretty good one. The Cowboys made a late run at the Steelers, but fell 21–17 in a well-played contest between two teams that deserved to be there. There had been speculation prior to the big game that Steelers star WR Lynn Swann wouldn't play. He had suffered a concussion in the AFC Championship against the Raiders that put him in the hospital.

But, oh yeah, Swann played. QB Terry Bradshaw hit him on long routes multiple times, including the grab

Swann is most famous for, an all-out, fingertip catch over Dallas cornerback (CB) Mark Washington. Sorry, Dallas. And sorry, all sons of the Lone Star State. **Tyler can't compete with Super Bowl X in this matchup.**

SUPER BOWL X

SCORE: Pittsburgh Steelers 21, Dallas Cowboys 17 **DATE:** January 18, 1976
LOCATION: Orange Bowl, Miami, FL
REGULAR SEASON RECORDS: Steelers 12–2, Cowboys 10–4
GAME MVP: Steelers WR Lynn Swann **TV AUDIENCE:** 57.7 million
COST OF 30-SECOND COMMERCIAL: $110,000

★ *Score After this Match* ★	
PRESIDENTS	7
SUPER BOWLS	3
QUARTER	○ ● ● ●

JAMES POLK

HOME STATE: Tennessee **PARTY:** Democratic
DATES AS PRESIDENT: 1845–1849
AGE AS PRESIDENT: 49 **REASON LEFT OFFICE:** Retired
ELECTORAL VOTES: 1844: Polk 170, Clay 105

Polk was really into the one-term presidency. In fact, he wrongly said, "I predict that no president of the United States, of either party, will ever again be re-elected."

Here's what you can say about James Knox Polk: **He went out there and got it done.**

And don't you forget it!

The eleventh president made the most of a single term in office, from 1845 to 1849; then he waved to fans and walked off without dragging out his exit. Take that, Brett Favre. Polk established a federal treasury and opened the U.S. Naval Academy and Smithsonian Institution. During his tenure three useful states entered the union: Texas, Iowa, and Wisconsin. Polk Nation won the Mexican-American War, too, nabbing California, Arizona, and much of the rest of the West as future U.S. states. Years later in Pasadena, the Vikings couldn't even get it done once. They lost their fourth Super Bowl. It was just getting sad. This

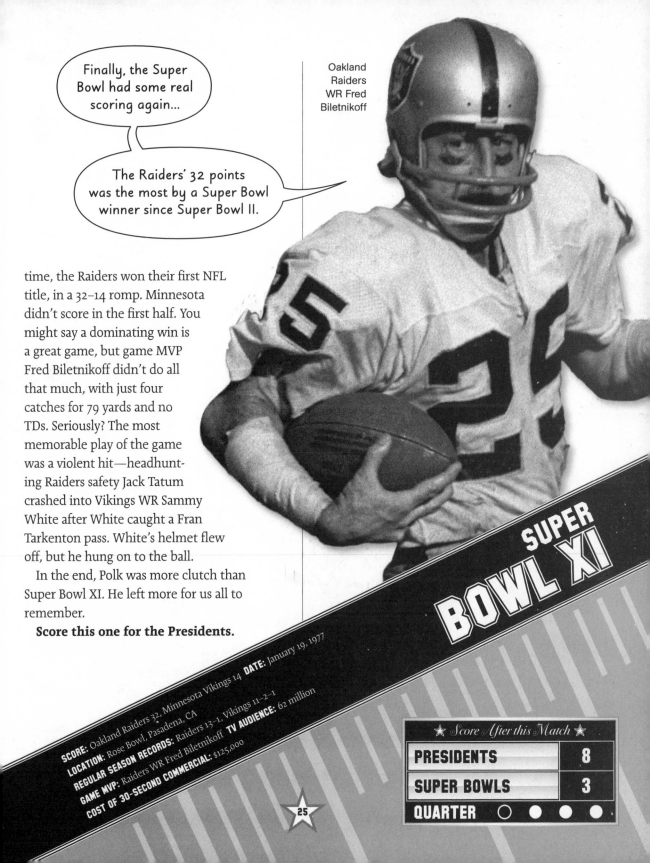

Finally, the Super Bowl had some real scoring again...

The Raiders' 32 points was the most by a Super Bowl winner since Super Bowl II.

Oakland Raiders WR Fred Biletnikoff

time, the Raiders won their first NFL title, in a 32–14 romp. Minnesota didn't score in the first half. You might say a dominating win is a great game, but game MVP Fred Biletnikoff didn't do all that much, with just four catches for 79 yards and no TDs. Seriously? The most memorable play of the game was a violent hit—headhunting Raiders safety Jack Tatum crashed into Vikings WR Sammy White after White caught a Fran Tarkenton pass. White's helmet flew off, but he hung on to the ball.

In the end, Polk was more clutch than Super Bowl XI. He left more for us all to remember.

Score this one for the Presidents.

SUPER BOWL XI

SCORE: Oakland Raiders 32, Minnesota Vikings 14 **DATE:** January 19, 1977
LOCATION: Rose Bowl, Pasadena, CA
REGULAR SEASON RECORDS: Raiders 13–1, Vikings 11–2–1
GAME MVP: Raiders WR Fred Biletnikoff **TV AUDIENCE:** 62 million
COST OF 30-SECOND COMMERCIAL: $125,000

★ *Score After this Match* ★

PRESIDENTS	8
SUPER BOWLS	3
QUARTER	○ ● ● ●

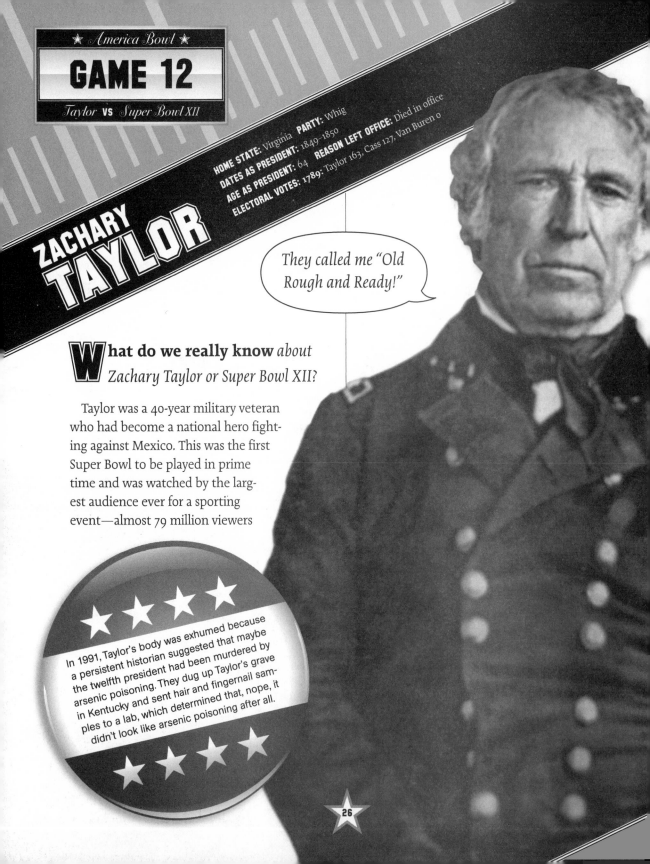

HOME STATE: Virginia **PARTY:** Whig
DATES AS PRESIDENT: 1849–1850
AGE AS PRESIDENT: 64 **REASON LEFT OFFICE:** Died in office
ELECTORAL VOTES: 1789: Taylor 163, Cass 127, Van Buren 0

ZACHARY TAYLOR

> *They called me "Old Rough and Ready!"*

What do we really know *about Zachary Taylor or Super Bowl XII?*

Taylor was a 40-year military veteran who had become a national hero fighting against Mexico. This was the first Super Bowl to be played in prime time and was watched by the largest audience ever for a sporting event—almost 79 million viewers

In 1991, Taylor's body was exhumed because a persistent historian suggested that maybe the twelfth president had been murdered by arsenic poisoning. They dug up Taylor's grave in Kentucky and sent hair and fingernail samples to a lab, which determined that, nope, it didn't look like arsenic poisoning after all.

in the U.S. and more than 100 million world-wide.

Taylor was known as "Old Rough and Ready" because he was up for anything, and because nicknames back then often started with "Old" regardless of age. The game matched Dallas's "Doomsday Defense" against Denver's "Orange Crush."

Taylor was in office for about 16 months: on July 4, 1850, he attended a ceremony connected with the construction of the Washington Monument. He felt hot, reportedly, so he drank lots of water, then ate cherries, and drank "iced milk." That night he got gastroenteritis and a fever. He died on July 9. But prior to dying, Taylor had done most of the legwork to get California admitted to the United States as a non-slave state.

The big game was sloppy—it featured ten fumbles and four interceptions (INTs), all of the INTs thrown by Broncos QB Craig Morton. Denver didn't score in the first half, and the result was never much in doubt, as the Cowboys won easily, 27–10. For a game that so many people watched, it was a pretty poor excuse for entertainment. That's 1978 network prime time for you.

Who wins? Look at it this way: If you could live through either another Taylor presidency or another Cowboys Super Bowl blowout, which would you choose? Think hard. That's right. We're thinking ABC: Anything But Cowboys.

Victory Taylor.

In case the Cowboys weren't enough Texas for people in 1978, the TV show *Dallas* premiered later in the year.

It was on CBS, just like the Super Bowl.

Dallas's J.R. Ewing, as played by Larry Hagman

SUPER BOWL XII

SCORE: Dallas Cowboys 27, Denver Broncos 10 **DATE:** January 15, 1978
LOCATION: Louisiana Superdome, New Orleans, LA
REGULAR SEASON RECORDS: Cowboys 12–2, Broncos 12–2
GAME MVP: Cowboys defensive tackle (DT) Randy White and defensive end (DE) Harvey Martin
TV AUDIENCE: 78.94 million **COST OF 30-SECOND COMMERCIAL:** $162,000

★ *Score After this Match* ★

PRESIDENTS	9
SUPER BOWLS	3
QUARTER	● ○ ● ●

MILLARD FILLMORE

HOME STATE: New York **PARTY**: Whig
DATES AS PRESIDENT: 1850–1853
AGE AS PRESIDENT: 50 **REASON LEFT OFFICE**: Retired
ELECTORAL VOTES: 1856: Buchanan 174, Fremont 114, Fillmore 8

> The 1850 Compromise got California into the union as a free state, which—I must say—was quite good.

Millard Fillmore, right? **No respect.**

Fillmore was never elected president. He snuck into office when Taylor passed away in 1850. No one saw it coming. Then Fillmore didn't even get his party's nomination when the next election came around. He was the last Whig to be a president. As part of the Compromise of 1850, he signed the Fugitive Slave Act, which declared that all runaway slaves be brought back to their masters. No one is suggesting that Fillmore should have a nice bowl of cherries and iced milk. But, for crying out loud, we can do better.

With Super Bowl XIII, the game was becoming a truly super event. The TV audience was soaring, and here was a matchup of two great teams. The winner would become the first three-time Super Bowl champ. The Steelers and Cowboys both scored on TD passes in the first quarter. The Cowboys went ahead 14–7 on a fumble return by linebacker Mike Hegman. Then, before the half, the Steelers took a 21–14 lead with two more Terry Bradshaw TD passes, including a 75-yard strike to John Stallworth.

Dallas almost made it close with two unanswered TDs in the fourth quarter to bring the score to 35–31. But time ran out. Unlike Fillmore, this game had its own goat: Dallas's Hall of Fame tight end (TE) Jackie Smith, who dropped a pass in the end zone in the third quarter, forcing the Cowboys to settle for a field goal instead of a TD, in a game the Boys lost by four points. Ouch! Smith retired before the next season and is believed to be the last Whig tight end in Cowboys history. **This hard-fought victory goes to the Super Bowl.**

Smith was still one of the greats. His 212 receiving yards in one game in 1963 were the record for a tight end until Shannon Sharpe had 214 in a 2002 game.

How could I drop that pass?!

Dallas Cowboys TE Jackie Smith

SUPER BOWL XIII

SCORE: Pittsburgh Steelers 35, Dallas Cowboys 31 **DATE:** January 21, 1979
LOCATION: Orange Bowl, Miami, FL
REGULAR SEASON RECORDS: Steelers 14-2, Cowboys 12-4
GAME MVP: Steelers QB Terry Bradshaw **TV AUDIENCE:** 74.74 million
COST OF 30-SECOND COMMERCIAL: $185,000

★ *Score After this Match* ★

PRESIDENTS	9
SUPER BOWLS	4
QUARTER	● ○ ● ●

FRANKLIN PIERCE

HOME STATE: New Hampshire **PARTY:** Democratic
DATES AS PRESIDENT: 1853–1857
AGE AS PRESIDENT: 48 **REASON LEFT OFFICE:** Not nominated for re-election
ELECTORAL VOTES: 1852: Pierce 254, Scott 42

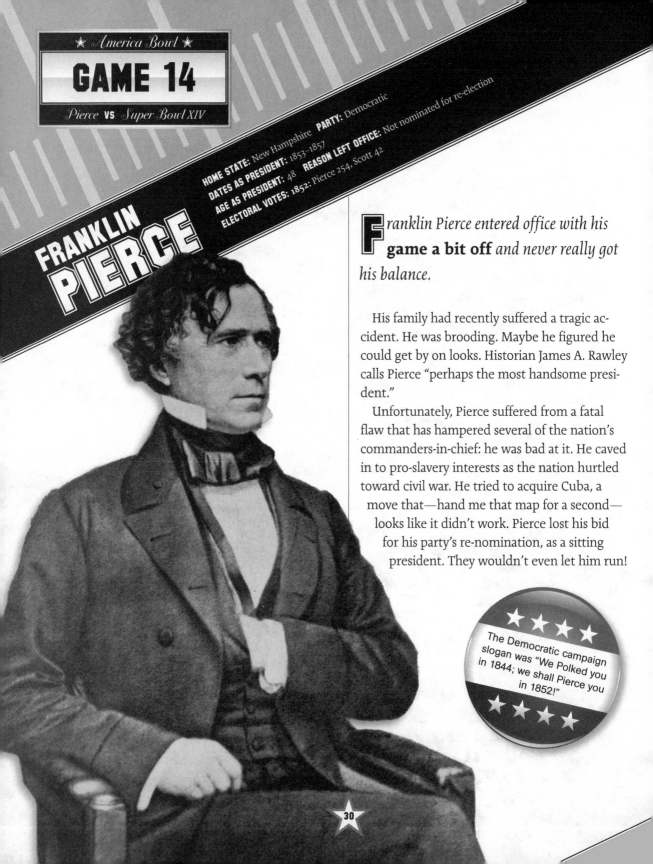

Franklin Pierce entered office with his **game a bit off** *and never really got his balance.*

His family had recently suffered a tragic accident. He was brooding. Maybe he figured he could get by on looks. Historian James A. Rawley calls Pierce "perhaps the most handsome president."

Unfortunately, Pierce suffered from a fatal flaw that has hampered several of the nation's commanders-in-chief: he was bad at it. He caved in to pro-slavery interests as the nation hurtled toward civil war. He tried to acquire Cuba, a move that—hand me that map for a second—looks like it didn't work. Pierce lost his bid for his party's re-nomination, as a sitting president. They wouldn't even let him run!

★ ★ ★ ★
The Democratic campaign slogan was "We Polked you in 1844; we shall Pierce you in 1852!"
★ ★ ★ ★

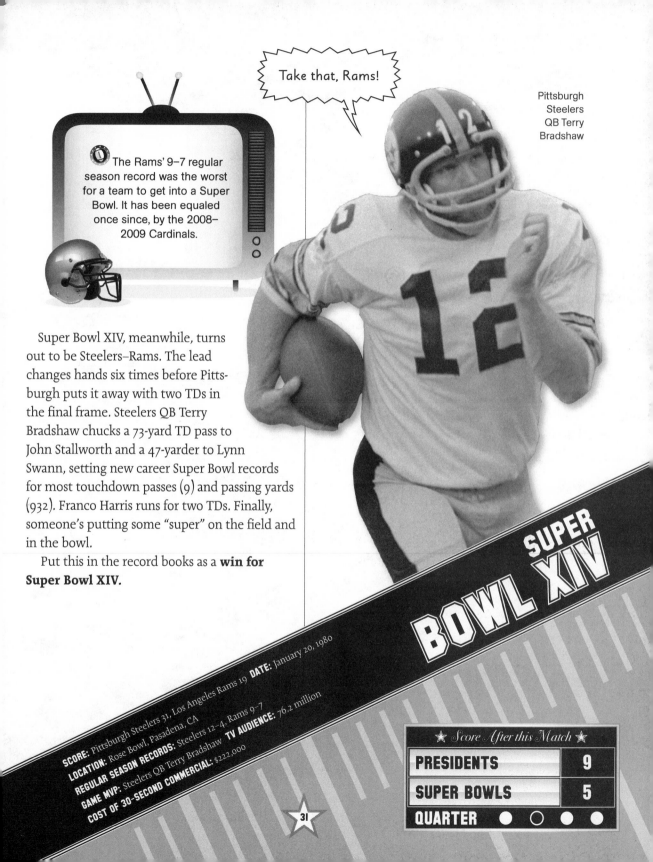

> Take that, Rams!

The Rams' 9–7 regular season record was the worst for a team to get into a Super Bowl. It has been equaled once since, by the 2008–2009 Cardinals.

Pittsburgh Steelers QB Terry Bradshaw

Super Bowl XIV, meanwhile, turns out to be Steelers–Rams. The lead changes hands six times before Pittsburgh puts it away with two TDs in the final frame. Steelers QB Terry Bradshaw chucks a 73-yard TD pass to John Stallworth and a 47-yarder to Lynn Swann, setting new career Super Bowl records for most touchdown passes (9) and passing yards (932). Franco Harris runs for two TDs. Finally, someone's putting some "super" on the field and in the bowl.

Put this in the record books as a **win for Super Bowl XIV.**

SUPER BOWL XIV

SCORE: Pittsburgh Steelers 31, Los Angeles Rams 19 **DATE:** January 20, 1980
LOCATION: Rose Bowl, Pasadena, CA
REGULAR SEASON RECORDS: Steelers 12–4, Rams 9–7 **TV AUDIENCE:** 76.2 million
GAME MVP: Steelers QB Terry Bradshaw
COST OF 30-SECOND COMMERCIAL: $222,000

★ *Score After this Match* ★

PRESIDENTS	9
SUPER BOWLS	5
QUARTER	● ○ ● ●

HOME STATE: Pennsylvania **PARTY:** Democratic
DATES AS PRESIDENT: 1857–1861 **REASON LEFT OFFICE:** Retired
AGE AS PRESIDENT: 65
ELECTORAL VOTES: 1856: Buchanan 174, Fremont 114, Fillmore 8

JAMES BUCHANAN

Yes, it is true . . . I am the only president to have never married!

The Eagles, like James Buchanan, came all the way from Pennsylvania to the nation's biggest stage, only to **embarrass themselves.**

The Raiders stormed to a first-quarter 14–0 lead over Philly in Super Bowl XV, and that was all the black-and-silver horde needed to go home with the Lombardi trophy. Dick Vermeil's birds just couldn't rise to the occasion. Eagles QB Ron Jaworski went 18 for 38 with three interceptions. Raiders QB Jim Plunkett threw for three touchdowns, two of them airmailed via his "branch office," Cliff Branch. Very nice performance. It ended 27–10. But if the measure of a good game is its competitiveness, this one was too small to measure without the aid of modern nanotechnology.

On the other hand,

Buchanan choked. A 2009 C-SPAN poll ranked Buchanan last place among presidents. He presided over the nation's plunge toward civil war. He promised not to run again *in his inaugural address.* Then he gladly got out of Dodge when Lincoln took over. *I'm outta here, Abe! See you on the History Channel!*

This clash of mediocrity cannot be settled in regulation time. We extend into overtime, where, according to America Bowl rules (which have just been made up on this page), we consider the intangibles. After the Super Bowl, NFL commissioner Pete Rozelle had to force a smile for the cameras while he handed the championship trophy to Al Davis, whom he'd hated ever since their bitter NFL–AFL rivalry. You have to love such a classic post-game moment.

Score another point for the Super Bowls.

My TD throw that *wasn't* to Cliff Branch was a clutch pass while scrambling to RB Kenny King.

King took it home for a then-Super-Bowl-record 80-yard touchdown.

You go Kenny!

Oakland Raiders
QB Jim Plunkett

SUPER BOWL XV

SCORE: Oakland Raiders 27, Philadelphia Eagles 10 **DATE:** January 25, 1981
LOCATION: Louisiana Superdome, New Orleans, LA
REGULAR SEASON RECORDS: Raiders 11–5, Eagles 12–4
GAME MVP: Raiders QB Jim Plunkett **TV AUDIENCE:** 68.29 million
COST OF 30-SECOND COMMERCIAL: $324,000

★ *Score After this Match* ★

PRESIDENTS	9
SUPER BOWLS	6
QUARTER	● ○ ● ●

DID YOU KNOW that "Honest Abe" Lincoln is the country's tallest president? **He was a whopping 6'4"!**

ABRAHAM LINCOLN

HOME STATE: Illinois **PARTY:** Republican
DATES AS PRESIDENT: 1861–1865
AGE AS PRESIDENT: 52 **REASON LEFT OFFICE:** Assassinated
ELECTORAL VOTES: 1860: Lincoln 180, Breckinridge 72, Bell 39, Douglas 12
1864: Lincoln 212, McClellan 21

Joe Montana led the 49ers to an impressive 26–21 win over the Bengals, passing for one TD and running for one—**but he didn't free the slaves.**

The game was among the most widely watched television broadcasts in American history, and it featured the debut of the Telestrator—but it didn't hold a fractured nation together through a Civil War. San Francisco's 20–0 half-

The Emancipation Proclamation, an order by President Lincoln in 1862, declared freedom for many American slaves and set a course for all slaves to become free and slavery to be outlawed in the Unites States.

34

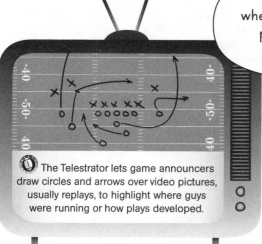

The Telestrator lets game announcers draw circles and arrows over video pictures, usually replays, to highlight where guys were running or how plays developed.

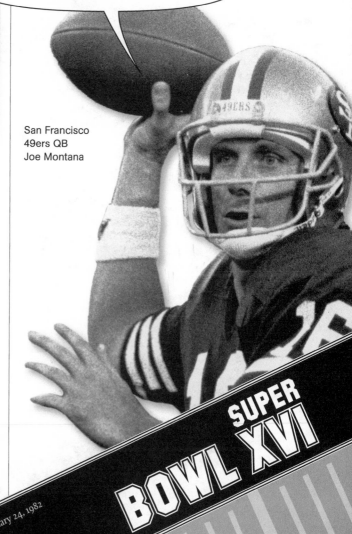

San Francisco got into the Super Bowl when I threw a back–of–the–end–zone TD pass to Dwight Clark that has been immortalized as "The Catch."

San Francisco
49ers QB
Joe Montana

time lead was the largest shutout lead at half-time in Super Bowl history—but it didn't deliver The Gettysburg Address.

Look, we could go on. We could figure out some formula to prove that fourscore and seven years beats two touchdowns and four field goals. But hey, the world will little note, nor long re-member, what we say here. Super Bowl XVI was pretty good. President 16 was pretty great.

With malice toward none—and in this we include the Bengals—**it's Abraham Lincoln in a walkover.**

SUPER BOWL XVI

SCORE: San Francisco 49ers 35, Cincinnati Bengals 21 **DATE:** January 24, 1982
LOCATION: Pontiac Silverdome, Pontiac, MI
REGULAR SEASON RECORDS: 49ers 13–3, Bengals 12–4
GAME MVP: 49ers QB Joe Montana **TV AUDIENCE:** 85.24 million
COST OF 30-SECOND COMMERCIAL: $324,000

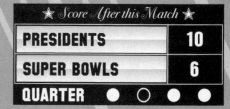

★ *Score After this Match* ★

PRESIDENTS	10
SUPER BOWLS	6

QUARTER ● ○ ● ●

HOME STATE: North Carolina **PARTY:** Democratic
DATES AS PRESIDENT: 1865–1869 **REASON LEFT OFFICE:** Retired
AGE AS PRESIDENT: 56
ELECTORAL VOTES: None

ANDREW JOHNSON

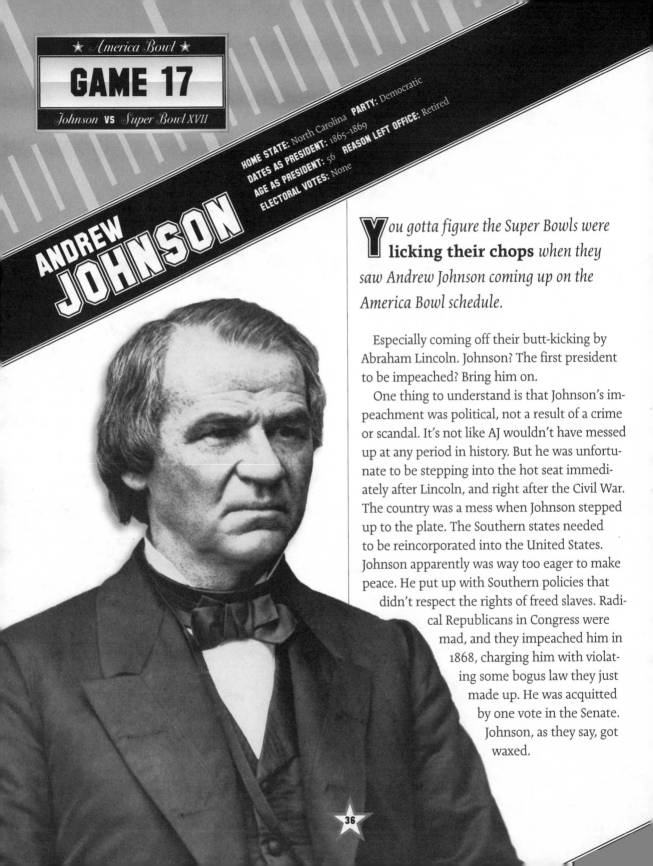

You gotta figure the Super Bowls were **licking their chops** when they saw Andrew Johnson coming up on the America Bowl schedule.

Especially coming off their butt-kicking by Abraham Lincoln. Johnson? The first president to be impeached? Bring him on.

One thing to understand is that Johnson's impeachment was political, not a result of a crime or scandal. It's not like AJ wouldn't have messed up at any period in history. But he was unfortunate to be stepping into the hot seat immediately after Lincoln, and right after the Civil War. The country was a mess when Johnson stepped up to the plate. The Southern states needed to be reincorporated into the United States. Johnson apparently was way too eager to make peace. He put up with Southern policies that didn't respect the rights of freed slaves. Radical Republicans in Congress were mad, and they impeached him in 1868, charging him with violating some bogus law they just made up. He was acquitted by one vote in the Senate. Johnson, as they say, got waxed.

Super Bowl XVII didn't need to be an ESPN Classic to beat that. After a weird, strike-shortened, nine-game season, the Redskins took their first NFL title, beating the Dolphins 27–17. The game was tight. Miami led at the half, scoring early on two super-long plays including Fulton Walker's 98-yard kick-return TD, the first in Super Bowl history. Then Washington's Hogs took over. They blew Miami off the line of scrimmage and brought forth a pounding old-school running attack. RB John Riggins sealed the deal on a fourth-and-one in the fourth quarter, bouncing off a tackler to the left and breaking free for a 43-yard TD run, en route to breaking the Super Bowl game rushing record with 166 yards.

The Redskins' tough, grunting offensive line was nicknamed "the Hogs." They pretty much still are. The name inspired a regular group of male fans to attend games as the "Hogettes," wearing women's clothing and pig snouts. This is actually true.

There's only one song to sing after this one: **Hail to the ~~Chief~~ Redskins!**

Super Bowl XVII was a rematch—and a revenge. The Fins had beaten the Skins in Super Bowl VII.

ARGH!

SUPER BOWL XVII

SCORE: Washington Redskins 27, Miami Dolphins 17 **DATE:** January 30, 1983
LOCATION: Rose Bowl, Pasadena, CA
REGULAR SEASON RECORDS: Redskins 8–1, Dolphins 7–2
GAME MVP: Redskins RB John Riggins **TV AUDIENCE:** 81.77 million
COST OF 30-SECOND COMMERCIAL: $400,000

★ *Score After this Match* ★	
PRESIDENTS	10
SUPER BOWLS	7
QUARTER	● ○ ● ●

HOME STATE: Ohio **PARTY:** Republican
DATES AS PRESIDENT: 1869–1877
AGE AS PRESIDENT: 46 **REASON LEFT OFFICE:** Retired
ELECTORAL VOTES: 1868: Grant 214, Seymour 80
1872: Grant 286, Greeley 0

ULYSSES S. GRANT

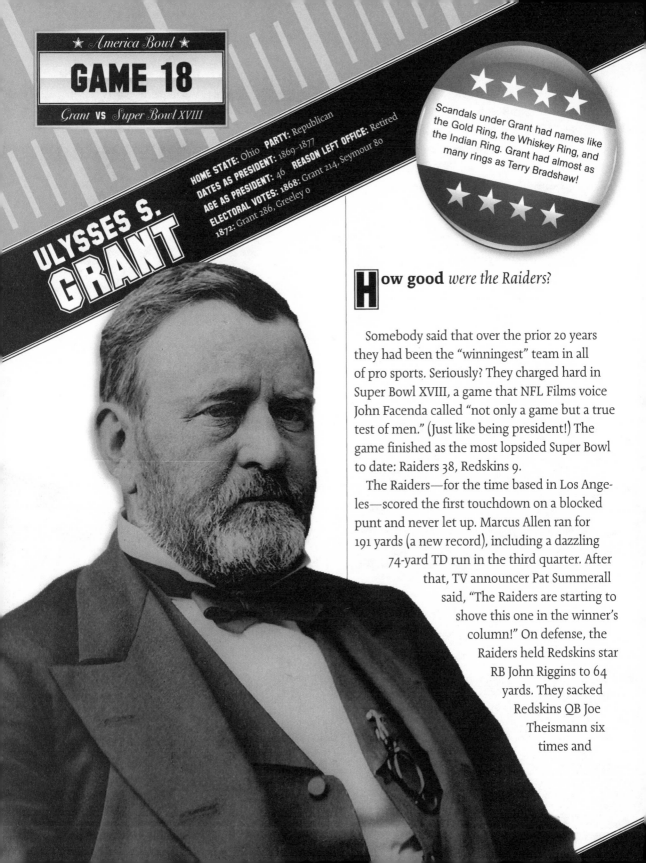

Scandals under Grant had names like the Gold Ring, the Whiskey Ring, and the Indian Ring. Grant had almost as many rings as Terry Bradshaw!

How good *were the Raiders?*

Somebody said that over the prior 20 years they had been the "winningest" team in all of pro sports. Seriously? They charged hard in Super Bowl XVIII, a game that NFL Films voice John Facenda called "not only a game but a true test of men." (Just like being president!) The game finished as the most lopsided Super Bowl to date: Raiders 38, Redskins 9.

The Raiders—for the time based in Los Angeles—scored the first touchdown on a blocked punt and never let up. Marcus Allen ran for 191 yards (a new record), including a dazzling 74-yard TD run in the third quarter. After that, TV announcer Pat Summerall said, "The Raiders are starting to shove this one in the winner's column!" On defense, the Raiders held Redskins star RB John Riggins to 64 yards. They sacked Redskins QB Joe Theismann six times and intercepted him twice. That included a deadly dagger by one-hit-wonder Jack Squirek, a reserve linebacker who, inserted for a single play by coaches who anticipated a Washington screen pass, picked off the pass and loped into the end zone.

Ulysses S. Grant was a war hero for the Union army but hardly a super president. He associated with the wrong guys and listened to bad advice. His administration oversaw scandals the way a convenience store cashier oversees gum. But Grant did preside over Reconstruction and de-

From 1964 to 1983, the Raiders were 196–78. That's a .715 winning percentage. In the NHL, over the prior 20 full hockey seasons at the time of Super Bowl XVIII, the Montreal Canadiens had a .712 win rate, and in the NBA the Boston Celtics had a .647 win rate.

fended civil rights. He served two terms—even went for a three-peat (unsuccessfully). Look, we've had better. He probably wasn't the right man for a desk job. But Grant beat the pants off that mismatched Super Bowl game.

Shove this one in the **winner's column for the Presidents.**

We're number 1!

Los Angeles Raiders
RB Marcus Allen

SUPER BOWL XVIII

SCORE: Los Angeles Raiders 38, Washington Redskins 9 **DATE:** January 22, 1984
LOCATION: Tampa Stadium, Tampa, FL
REGULAR SEASON RECORDS: Raiders 12–4, Redskins 14–2
GAME MVP: Raiders RB Marcus Allen **TV AUDIENCE:** 77.62 million
COST OF 30-SECOND COMMERCIAL: $368,000

39

★ Score After this Match ★	
PRESIDENTS	11
SUPER BOWLS	7
QUARTER	● ○ ● ●

RUTHERFORD B. HAYES

HOME STATE: Ohio **PARTY:** Republican
DATES AS PRESIDENT: 1877–1881
AGE AS PRESIDENT: 54 **REASON LEFT OFFICE:** Retired
ELECTORAL VOTES: 1876: Hayes 185, Tilden 184

I'm no fraud!

Rutherford B. Hayes and Super Bowl XIX had **hated each other for years.**

Super Bowl XIX taunted Hayes for losing the popular vote of 1876 and weaseling into office by one measly electoral vote. Hayes, in turn, labeled the 1985 game, in which the 49ers beat the Dolphins 38–16, "immeasurably calamitous." There was some serious bad blood.

The election of 1876 was riddled with corruption. Vote counts were seriously messed up in Florida, Louisiana, and South Carolina. Things ultimately were settled by a congressional committee, whose Republican majority favored Hayes. Some observers protested by calling the new president "Rutherfraud Hayes."

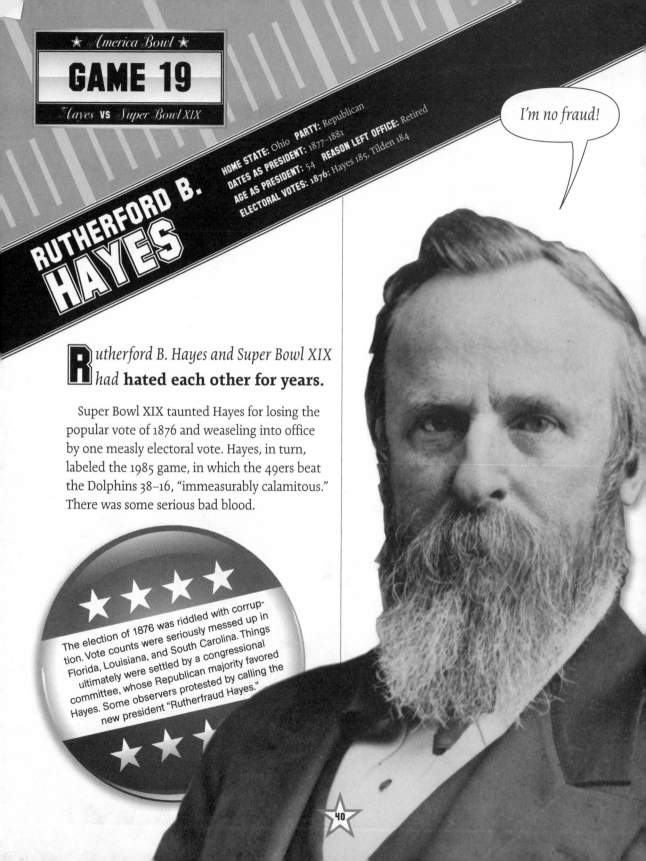

OK, not really—I'm just trying to inject some pre-game excitement into this snoozer of a matchup.

The game indeed wasn't that exciting. Niners QB Joe Montana was too good for Miami, passing for three TDs and a Super Bowl record 331 yards. Dolphins QB Dan Marino would lose in his only Super Bowl appearance.

President Hayes came in with a good game plan, but you know what they say: game plans go out the window the first time you get hit. Hayes went in seeking a fairer shake for Indians and former slaves. But the states and Congress foiled his intentions. He allowed racist Jim Crow laws to spread across the South. He sent federal troops to shoot at striking railroad workers.

Where did it go wrong? In the end Hayes could only blame himself.

Score one for the Super Bowls.

San Francisco 49ers QB Joe Montana

This Super Bowl, unusually, took place on January 20, the legal day on which a president is inaugurated. Ronald Reagan was sworn in for his second term on Super Bowl Sunday, privately in the White House grand foyer and had the usual public outdoor ceremony the day after.

SUPER BOWL XIX

SCORE: San Francisco 49ers 38, Miami Dolphins 16 **DATE:** January 20, 1985
LOCATION: Stanford Stadium, Stanford, CA
REGULAR SEASON RECORDS: 49ers 15–1, Dolphins 14–2
GAME MVP: 49ers QB Joe Montana **TV AUDIENCE:** 85.53 million
COST OF 30-SECOND COMMERCIAL: $525,000

★ *Score After this Match* ★

PRESIDENTS	11
SUPER BOWLS	8
QUARTER	● ○ ● ●

HOME STATE: Ohio PARTY: Republican
DATES AS PRESIDENT: 1881
AGE AS PRESIDENT: 49 REASON LEFT OFFICE: Assassinated
ELECTORAL VOTES: 1880: Garfield 214, Hancock 155

JAMES GARFIELD

We are the Bears Shufflin' Crew
Shufflin' on down, doin' it for you.
We're so bad we know we're good.
Blowin' your mind like we knew we would.
You know we're just struttin' for fun
Struttin' our stuff for everyone.
We're not here to start no trouble.
We're just here to do the Super Bowl Shuffle.

The American music scene in 1985 was not good. Stop me when I get to one of 1985's top songs that you want to hear again: "Careless Whisper," "Like a Virgin," "I Want to Know What Love Is," "Out of Touch," "Crazy for You," "Easy Lover," "Can't Fight This Feeling," "Saving All My Love for You," "Wake Me Up Before You Go Go," "The Power of Love," "You're the Inspiration." Right, it just gets worse. If you're too young to remember these songs, there's just one thing I can say to you: congratulations.

The members of the 1985 Chicago Bears who put on pads and game tights to record a music video or "Super Bowl Shuffle" probably figured, look, how bad could it be? We couldn't

Garfield escaped the chains of poverty as a child by reading and daydreaming. According to one biographer, Garfield left home at age 16 to become a sailor, worked on a canal boat for six weeks, and fell overboard 14 times—a record unbroken by any subsequent president.

possibly make something as soul-draining as "We Built This City" or "The Heat Is On." Well, they were wrong. In retrospect, the only plausible explanation is that the 1985 Bears were so confident about what they could do on the football field, they just didn't care what they looked like anywhere else.

The Bears went 15–1 during the regular season. They didn't allow a single point in either the divisional playoff or the NFC Championship game. Their defense was paced by nails-tough linebacker Mike Singletary and a 300-pound rookie defensive tackle nicknamed "the Refrigerator." The offense was driven by sassy QB Jim McMahon and Hall of Fame RB Walter Payton. Does anyone even recall who was on the Patriots? The Pats scored first in Super Bowl XX, but very quickly after that the game was gone. The Bears led 23–3 at the half and outscored New England 21–0 in the third quarter, the last of those TDs on a one-yard run by the Fridge himself. The game ended 46–10. There is something to be said for utter dominance, and also (in retrospect) for anything that humbles the Patriots. But this game was like a movie with interesting characters and a horrible script. You know, like Star Wars Episode 2: Attack of the Clones.

James Garfield was in office for a total of six months in 1881. Before that he was a really interesting guy. He read books and played sports. He was a college president at age

26. As a congressman before the Civil War, he wanted to free the slaves and confiscate slave-owners' estates. As president he made mistakes—there was questionable money he took for backing a certain government contract—but he was thoughtful. His big issue was money: that to be legitimate it needed to be tied to gold and not just printed up on whatever scrap paper the U.S. Mint had lying around. Then a disgruntled office seeker shot him. Hey, nobody's putting Garfield in the Hall of Fame. But all he really had to do was make it past the part where he swore "to the best of my ability" to **beat this clunker of a Super Bowl game.**

> A few team members, notably QB Jim McMahon, reunited for (hard to believe) an even worse remake, in a commercial for a mobile phone company that aired during Super Bowl XLIV in 2010.

Chicago Bears DE
Richard Dent

SUPER BOWL XX

SCORE: Chicago Bears 46, New England Patriots 10 **DATE:** January 26, 1986
LOCATION: Louisiana Superdome, New Orleans, LA
REGULAR SEASON RECORDS: Bears 15–1, Patriots 11–5
GAME MVP: Bears DE Richard Dent **TV AUDIENCE:** 92.57 million
COST OF 30-SECOND COMMERCIAL: $550,000

★ Score After this Match ★	
PRESIDENTS	12
SUPER BOWLS	8
QUARTER	● ○ ● ●

HOME STATE: Vermont **PARTY:** Republican
DATES AS PRESIDENT: 1881–1885
AGE AS PRESIDENT: 51 **REASON LEFT OFFICE:** Not nominated for re-election
ELECTORAL VOTES: None

CHESTER A. ARTHUR

Stop that music!

Every so often *a man is thrust into the spotlight unexpectedly.*

A few rise to the occasion and shine. Others do not. This is the story of one of each type, Phil Simms and Chester A. Arthur.

The 1986 Giants had dominated the NFC but had done it mostly on the ground. Halfback Joe Morris averaged more than 100 yards a game and finished third in the NFL in rushing.

Chester Arthur didn't even like the song "Hail to the Chief" and refused to have it played when he entered the room.

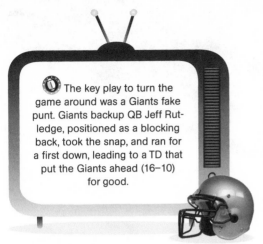

The key play to turn the game around was a Giants fake punt. Giants backup QB Jeff Rutledge, positioned as a blocking back, took the snap, and ran for a first down, leading to a TD that put the Giants ahead (16–10) for good.

bullet, and the cordial, mutton-chopped Arthur was pressed into duty. He was, by most accounts, adequate. He surprised critics who feared he'd be corrupt by not being as corrupt as they expected. But he never took his game to the next level.

Simms and Arthur. Some say it isn't really a fair comparison. But when all is said and done, and all the dice have been rolled, **this victory most clearly belongs to the Super Bowls.**

New York Giants QB Phil Simms and LB Lawrence Taylor celebrate

As quarterback for New York, Simms, in his seventh season, seemed like a journeyman. In the 1986 regular season he had a wobbly 74.6 passer rating and a workmanlike 55 percent completion rate. Yet in the Giants' first Super Bowl appearance, matched against Denver's young gunslinger John Elway, how Simms glowed. He completed 22 of 25 passes (88 percent, the Super Bowl's best ever) for three TDs and no interceptions. His passer rating of 150.9 doubled his regular-season mark. The Giants, who trailed 10–9 at halftime, came back to blast the Broncos 17–0 in the third quarter and win 39–20. Simms' star was born.

The Giants hadn't been in a league title game since losing the 1963 NFL Championship to Chicago.

Chester Arthur perhaps was not meant for such greatness. He'd been installed as vice president under James Garfield and was expected to maintain a low profile. Then in 1881, Garfield was slain by an assassin's

SCORE: New York Giants 39, Denver Broncos 20 **DATE:** January 25, 1987
LOCATION: Rose Bowl, Pasadena, CA
REGULAR SEASON RECORDS: Giants 14-2, Broncos 11-5
GAME MVP: Giants QB Phil Simms **TV AUDIENCE:** 87.2 million
COST OF 30-SECOND COMMERCIAL: $600,000

SUPER BOWL XXI

★ *Score After this Match* ★	
PRESIDENTS	12
SUPER BOWLS	9
QUARTER	● ○ ● ●

HOME STATE: New Jersey **PARTY:** Democratic

DATES AS PRESIDENT: 1885–1889 and 1893–1897

AGE AS PRESIDENT: 47 **REASON LEFT OFFICE:** Lost re-election (1888), retired (1896)

ELECTORAL VOTES: 1884: Cleveland 219, Blaine 182 **1888:** B. Harrison 233, Cleveland 168, **1892:** Cleveland 277, B. Harrison 145, Weaver 22

GROVER CLEVELAND

See you again real soon.

Not to confuse the point of our game, but this is as close as Cleveland has **gotten to a Super Bowl.**

Unfortunately, it's Grover Cleveland. Look, nothing against Grover Cleveland's presidency, in this case his first go-around in the White House. He put up decent numbers and remains in the record books. He won the popular vote three times—1884, 1888, and 1892. But Washington gets the better of President Cleveland here—and by Washington we mean the Redskins.

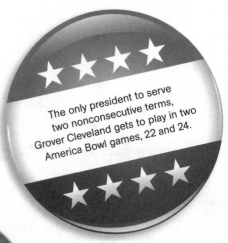

The only president to serve two nonconsecutive terms, Grover Cleveland gets to play in two America Bowl games, 22 and 24.

The Redskins broke all kinds of records while busting the Broncos 42–10. They set Super Bowl marks for most TDs in a game (6), most offensive yards (602), and most rushing yards (280), most of that running footage gained by unheralded rookie Timmy Smith, who put up a new Super Bowl rushing record with 204 yards (and two TDs). Redskins QB Doug Williams became the first African American QB to win a Super Bowl. Pretty good stuff. Sorry, Grover. **The Super Bowls pick up another America Bowl point here**—and now they're in striking distance.

Told you I was fast!

The Broncos had been preparing to defend the run against the big Redskins RB George Rogers, but the smaller, more agile Smith got the start instead, and he blew their minds.

Washington Redskins QB Doug Williams

SUPER BOWL XXII

SCORE: Washington Redskins 42, Denver Broncos 10 **DATE:** January 31, 1988
LOCATION: Jack Murphy Stadium, San Diego, CA
REGULAR SEASON RECORDS: Redskins 11–4, Broncos 10–4–1
GAME MVP: Redskins QB Doug Williams **TV AUDIENCE:** 80.14 million
COST OF 30-SECOND COMMERCIAL: $645,000

★ *Score After this Match* ★

PRESIDENTS	12
SUPER BOWLS	10
QUARTER	● ○ ● ●

HOME STATE: Indiana **PARTY:** Republican
DATES AS PRESIDENT: 1889–1893
AGE AS PRESIDENT: 55 **REASON LEFT OFFICE:** Lost re-election
ELECTORAL VOTES: 1888: B. Harrison 233, Cleveland 168
1892: Cleveland 277, B. Harrison 145, Weaver 22

BENJAMIN HARRISON

> *I was a little kid when my grandfather, William Henry Harrison was elected president.*

Time *does* **funny things.**

   It softens us up when we're alive. After we're gone, it can soften the reputations we leave behind. Benjamin Harrison for a long time was lumped in with all the late-1800s, post-Reconstruction presidents as a bunch of lawyers who didn't do much during a time when the nation slowly became more businesslike. He was called a "human iceberg." Teddy Roosevelt said of Harrison, "He is a cold-blooded,

★★★★ Ben Harrison is the only man ever to beat Grover Cleveland in a presidential election. ★★★★

narrow-minded, prejudiced, obstinate, timid psalm-singing Indianapolis politician." (Indianapolis, ouch. Maybe Teddy was thinking of Colts receiver *Marvin* Harrison). But time has done its business. Some modern historians give Ben Harrison high marks for making strides in foreign policy, like the time he set up Samoa as the first American protectorate, and advocated for a canal in Central America, and nailed down various other overseas treaties. It's something, anyway.

How has time treated Super Bowl XXIII? This 1989 game was representative of its time, a rematch between the 49ers and Bengals. But it was exceptionally super-duper. In a game that went down to the last minute, it was 49ers 20, Bengals 16. Cincinnati led three different times, once after a crazy 98-yard kickoff return by—Who?—Stanford Jennings. San Francisco kept tying the score but never held a lead until the final minute. Down 16–13 with about three minutes left, the 49ers took the ball at their own eight-yard line and went 92 yards in 11 plays, mostly passes from QB Joe Montana to WR Jerry Rice and RB Roger Craig. They took the lead on a 10-yard pass to WR John Taylor with 34 seconds remaining. It was a classic, a Super Bowl very worthy of the name.

Another Harrison bites the dust.

Joe Montana wasn't MVP, but he completed 23 of 36 passes for a Super Bowl record 357 yards.

San Francisco 49ers WR Jerrry Rice

C'mon boys!

Keep it up!

SUPER BOWL XXIII

SCORE: San Francisco 49ers 20, Cincinnati Bengals 16 **DATE:** January 22, 1989
LOCATION: Joe Robbie Stadium, Miami, FL
REGULAR SEASON RECORDS: 49ers 10–6, Bengals 12–4
GAME MVP: 49ers WR Jerry Rice **TV AUDIENCE:** 81.6 million
COST OF 30-SECOND COMMERCIAL: $675,000

★ *Score After this Match* ★

PRESIDENTS	12
SUPER BOWLS	11
QUARTER	● ● ○ ●

HOME STATE: New Jersey **PARTY:** Democratic
DATES AS PRESIDENT: 1885–1889 and 1893–1897
AGE AS PRESIDENT: 55 **REASON LEFT OFFICE:** Lost re-election (1888), retired (1896)
ELECTORAL VOTES: 1884: Cleveland 219, Blaine 182 **1888:** B. Harrison 233, Cleveland 168
1884: Cleveland 277, B. Harrison 145, Weaver 22

GROVER CLEVELAND

Grover Cleveland is pictured on the official U.S. 1,000 dollar bill. The government stopped making them in 2000.

H ere is what America lives for: the comeback.

As the twenty-second president, Grover Cleveland lost America Bowl Game 22, leaving the Presidents with a narrow two-point lead at halftime. Now, here he is, back in the saddle and gunning for revenge—as twenty-fourth president. Yes, Cleveland was the only U.S. president, in any weight class, to regain the title. He was twenty-second president from 1885 to 1889, then got robbed in 1888—he received the most votes for twenty-third president but lost by electoral vote to Benjamin Harrison. Now look who's back.

Super Bowl XXIV returned deep experience, too. Joe Montana, quarter-back for the 49ers, was 3–0 in Super Bowls already. Broncos QB John Elway was 0–2. By the time these two men were done, no quarterback had started more Super Bowl games. But could Elway come back from defeat and achieve vindication? Could Cleveland?

For Elway, well, apparently not. Super Bowl XXIV was the crushing slaughter that prior Broncos Super Bowls foretold. The Broncos entered the game with the NFL's best defense, but they couldn't prevent the 49ers from scoring two touchdowns in each quarter (that's eight total!), smashing all kinds of records en route to a 55–10 Bronco-bashing. Montana equaled Terry Bradshaw with a 4–0 lifetime Super Bowl tally. He became the first three-time Super Bowl MVP and set a new record with five TD passes before he was lifted from the game for 49ers backup Steve Young (who would later break that record). Elway would need to wait for his day.

Here was Cleveland's chance for redemption, matched against a lousy game. Could he do it? His second term began in 1893 with a stock market panic. Soon banks and railroads were closing and jobs were being lost. Cleveland thought it would help to repeal the Sherman Silver Purchase Act, taming inflation. In foreign policy, he stood his ground, forcing Britain to accept arbitration over some disputed territory in Venezuela. Cleveland didn't make much history in his return to the big stage. But in the end, he was more presidential than this Super Bowl was super.

Score a close one for the Presidents.

> Super Bowl XXIV's 55–10 final is the most lopsided Super Bowl score ever!

San Francisco 49ers WR Jerry Rice celebrates during Super Bowl XXIV

SUPER BOWL XXIV

SCORE: San Francisco 49ers 55, Denver Broncos 10 **DATE:** January 28, 1990
LOCATION: Louisiana Superdome, New Orleans, LA
REGULAR SEASON RECORDS: 49ers 14–2, Broncos 11–5
GAME MVP: 49ers QB Joe Montana **TV AUDIENCE:** 73.85 million
COST OF 30-SECOND COMMERCIAL: $700,000

★ *Score After this Match* ★

PRESIDENTS	13
SUPER BOWLS	11
QUARTER	● ● ○ ●

HOME STATE: Ohio **PARTY:** Republican
DATES AS PRESIDENT: 1897–1901
AGE AS PRESIDENT: 54 **REASON LEFT OFFICE:** Assassinated
ELECTORAL VOTES: 1896: McKinley 217, Bryan 176
1900: McKinley 292, Bryan 155

WILLIAM McKINLEY

McKinley was a big guy and always looking for ways to expand America. He annexed the Philippines, Puerto Rico, and Guam and set up a protectorate over Cuba.

Bigger is better!

The lesson of America Bowl Game 25 is a bitter one, but a lesson best not forgotten, a cautionary tale of how things that begin with success and promise can suddenly, unexpectedly, go wrong.

William McKinley, America's twenty-fifth president, was still celebrating the election to his second term in office when he was shockingly slain by an assassin. The Buffalo Bills rode into Super Bowl XXV seemingly untouchable, having won the AFC Championship game 51–3. Then they lost the Super Bowl when a field goal attempt by Scott Norwood sailed "wide right with eight seconds on the clock." The punch that hurts the most is the one you never saw coming.

The Bills indeed seemed unassailable. Their offense had scored the most points in the NFL during the 1990 regular season. QB Jim Kelly was the league's highest rated passer; RB Thurman Thomas was top NFL rusher. The defense was led by tenacious DE Bruce Smith, second in the NFL in sacks. The Bills were 13–3 in the regular season, and in squashing the Raiders in the AFC title game had six interceptions and seven touchdowns. They entered the Super Bowl as seven-point favorites over the Giants.

McKinley won the elections of 1896 and 1900 by giant margins, both times over multi-election loser William Jennings Bryan. McK's theme was "Prosperity at Home, Prestige Abroad." He worked hard on both. In 1898, Spain apparently sunk the USS *Maine*, and it was time for the Spanish-America War. At home, McKinley was pro-business, defending high tariffs to protect domestic producers (a stance he later relaxed) and defending the gold standard. The nation was in transition, becoming more industrial. In the end, when McKinley seemed to be sitting pretty, it was a disgruntled mill worker who shot him.

McKinley was not a bad chief exec, but Super Bowl XXV was a true test of wills that became more thrilling as it went on. The Bills led 12–10 at halftime, and then the lead started changing hands. The Giants pulled ahead 17–12 on an Ottis Anderson TD. The Bills went back out front 19–17 on a Thomas run. Matt Bahr's second field goal nudged the Giants back ahead 20–19. With the clock ticking down, the Bills drove downfield until the Giants stopped them at the 30-yard line with eight seconds left, and Norwood lined up for a 47-yard game-winning field goal. And it's . . . wide right. Game over. Giants win. An unexpected end for Buffalo, but an epic America-Bowl-point-winning game.

Look out, here come the Super Bowls.

The shocking missed field goal overshadowed some stellar individual performances in the game by Giants QB Jeff Hostetler and backs Ottis Anderson and Dave Meggett, as well as by Bills QB Jim Kelly and RB Thurman Thomas.

SUPER BOWL XXV

SCORE: New York Giants 20, Buffalo Bills 19 **DATE:** January 27, 1991
LOCATION: Tampa Stadium, Tampa, FL
REGULAR SEASON RECORDS: Giants 13–3, Bills 13–3 **TV AUDIENCE:** 79.51 million
GAME MVP: Giants RB Ottis Anderson
COST OF 30-SECOND COMMERCIAL: $800,000

★ *Score After this Match* ★

PRESIDENTS	13
SUPER BOWLS	12
QUARTER	● ● ○ ●

HOME STATE: New York **PARTY:** Republican
DATES AS PRESIDENT: 1901–1909
AGE AS PRESIDENT: 42 **REASON LEFT OFFICE:** Didn't seek re-election in 1908
ELECTORAL VOTES: 1904: Roosevelt 336, Parker 140
1912: Wilson 435, Roosevelt 88, Taft 8

THEODORE ROOSEVELT

Scene 1: Circa 1883. *Theodore Roosevelt is in a field with a rifle, killing buffalo.*

I am the youngest man in history to become U.S. president, a record I still hold, followed in order by Kennedy, Clinton, Grant, and Obama.

Scene 2: Super Bowl XXVI in 1992. Washington is on the field, killing Buffalo.

Scene 3: September 5, 1901. William McKinley, the twenty-fifth president of the United States, is in Buffalo, N.Y., attending an exposition. There's a man with a gun over there! McKinley is shot and killed. Vice president Theodore Roosevelt is rushed to Buffalo, where he is sworn in as U.S. president number 26. Then he goes to Washington.

Stranger things have

happened in America than this bizarre and somewhat macabre confluence of Buffalo-linked events. But not many. We're still putting the pieces together. We do know that at one point, after he got to Washington, President Roosevelt threatened to ban football. At the time, people said it was because he believed the sport was too violent.

Washington Redskins QB Mark Rypien

Super Bowl XXVI was a Buffalo slaughter, a disaster for the Bills. The Redskins were up 17–0 at halftime and 24–0 before the Bills even got on the scoreboard. Only two meaningless Buffalo touchdowns in the last quarter, putting the final tally at 37–24, made the game even seem close. Or were those TDs meaningless?

Teddy Roosevelt's achievements in office from 1901 to 1909 have been well documented by the authorities. He was wildly popular and used his "bully pulpit" to advocate strong action and get results. He took on big business monopolies and busted those trusts. He conserved 150 million acres of national forest and the wildlife living in it. He initiated construction of the Panama Canal and won a Nobel Peace Prize for arbitrating the end of the Russo-Japanese War. At least for our purposes here, there is no mystery. Send this case to the X-Files, but put it in the **winner's column for the Presidents.**

SUPER BOWL XXVI

SCORE: Washington Redskins 37, Buffalo Bills 24 **DATE:** January 26, 1992
LOCATION: Hubert H. Humphrey Metrodome, Minneapolis, MN
REGULAR SEASON RECORDS: Redskins 14-2, Bills 13-3 **TV AUDIENCE:** 79.6 million
GAME MVP: Redskins QB Mark Rypien
COST OF 30-SECOND COMMERCIAL: $850,000

★ Score After this Match ★	
PRESIDENTS	14
SUPER BOWLS	12
QUARTER	● ● ○ ●

★ America Bowl ★

GAME 27

Taft **VS** *Super Bowl XXVII*

WILLIAM HOWARD TAFT

HOME STATE: Ohio **PARTY:** Republican
DATES AS PRESIDENT: 1909–1913
AGE AS PRESIDENT: 51 **REASON LEFT OFFICE:** Lost re-election
ELECTORAL VOTES: 1908: Taft 321, Bryan 172
1912: Wilson 435, Roosevelt 88, Taft 8

Under Taft's administration the Sixteenth Amendment to the Constitution was passed, instituting an income tax for corporations.

Life isn't fair.

The monumental Super Bowl III drew its America Bowl match against the monument-inspiring Thomas Jefferson. It's a shame either of them had to lose. Now the mediocre twenty-seventh president William H. Taft is matched against one of the lamest Super Bowl games ever, the Cowboys' 52–17 slaughter of the Bills in Super Bowl XXVII. It's a shame either of them has to win.

There is really little to recommend the ballgame. Buffalo would lose its third straight Super Bowl. The Bills turned the ball over a record nine

I was the last president to have any facial hair at all. Go figure...

56

times, making the Dallas win too easy. Bills QB Jim Kelly was injured in the first half and left the game. The second Bills touchdown shouldn't even have counted because backup QB Frank Reich clearly had a foot over the line of scrimmage when he threw it. Cowboys QB Troy Aikman actually ran for more yards than Bills RB Thurman Thomas. Near the merciful end, Cowboys DT Leon Lett picked up a fumble and was about to make the score 58–17, but angry Bills WR Don Beebe raced up to him and smacked the ball out of his hand at the one-yard line. That's the kind of game it was. Just a frustrating smack.

Taft was no thriller, either. He's famous for, well, being obese. He report-

It looked like the Bills were a team of destiny—before this game started. They had engineered a shocking comeback from a 35–3 deficit to beat Houston in the AFC wild-card playoff game.

edly ate a dozen eggs, a pound of bacon, and a stack of pancakes for breakfast. And then it was lunchtime. But, by coming between Roosevelt and Wilson, all Taft really needed to do was fill the space for four years. Oh, he sure did. Life isn't fair. Again we ask the tiebreaker question: If you had to relive either the Taft years or Super Bowl XXVII, which would you choose?

We award this point to the Presidents.

Dallas Cowboys QB Troy Alkman

SUPER BOWL XXVII

SCORE: Dallas Cowboys 52, Buffalo Bills 17 **DATE:** January 31, 1993
LOCATION: Rose Bowl, Pasadena, CA
REGULAR SEASON RECORDS: Cowboys 13–3, Bills 11–5
GAME MVP: Cowboys QB Troy Aikman **TV AUDIENCE:** 90.99 million
COST OF 30-SECOND COMMERCIAL: $850,000

★ Score After this Match ★	
PRESIDENTS	15
SUPER BOWLS	12
QUARTER ● ● ○ ●	

WOODROW WILSON

HOME STATE: Virginia **PARTY:** Democratic
DATES AS PRESIDENT: 1913–1921
AGE AS PRESIDENT: 56 **REASON LEFT OFFICE:** Retired
ELECTORAL VOTES: 1912: Wilson 435, Roosevelt 88, Taft 8
1916: Wilson 277, Hughes 254

Every so often in life *there occurs an unfathomable coincidence that makes you say: "Uh, OK."*

In 1913, Thomas Woodrow Wilson became the twenty-eighth president of the United States. That same year, Thomas E. Wilson, a completely separate person, became president of a Chicago meatpacking company called Morris & Co. Also in 1913, Ashland Manufacturing Co., a business created to market leather from slaughterhouses, was formed. Stay with me. In 1915, Thomas E. Wilson was appointed president of Ashland, and by 1931 the business's name had changed to the Wilson Sporting Goods Co. After World War II, Wilson himself worked with football great Knute Rockne to develop a football made from the finest leather, with lock-stitch seams and triple lining. The Wilson ball eventually was adopted by the National Football League and used, among other places, to play Super Bowl XXVIII in 1994.

Now flash back to 1918, while Woodrow Wilson was serving his second term. Somewhere else completely Ralph J. Wilson Jr. was born. After World War II, Ralph Wilson formed Wilson Industries and later bought into the fledgling American Football League, becoming the owner of the Buffalo Bills. By 1994 the Bills had lost three consecutive Super Bowls and were heading into their fourth in a row. That's right, Super Bowl XXVIII, a rematch against the Dallas Cowboys. Get that ball ready.

Flash back to Woodrow Wilson. He got off to a quick start. In 1913, he created the Federal Reserve System. He strengthened antitrust laws and set up a graduated income tax. Then war broke out in Europe in 1914, and though no one realized it at first, it was World War I. By the time the United States got involved in 1917, the war was almost over. Wilson sought to create a League of Nations to ensure world peace, but he wouldn't compromise on the details, and when it finally

happened the United States didn't even join. Its problems led to another rematch: World War II.

The Bills got off to a quick start, too. In the first quarter, kicker Steve Christie hit a 54-yard field goal—a Super Bowl record. An 80-yard touchdown drive put the Bills ahead 10–6, and an interception led to a FG that had Buffalo on top 13–6 at the half. Then the war gods raged and Buffalo faltered once again. Less than a minute into the second half, Dallas took a Thurman Thomas fumble in for a game-tying TD. The rout was on. The Cowboys won 30–13, and the Bills became the only team in pro sports history to lose four straight championship games. After that the Bills were not in the Super Bowl again. Thankfully.

> Ralph Wilson Jr. is one of 12 people in the Pro Football Hall of Fame to have the last name of a U.S. president. Try to guess them all—or see this book's appendix for the list.

> With their second straight Super Bowl win, the Cowboys staked an early claim as "Team of the 1990s."

Dallas Cowboys
RB Emmit Smith

You might say that, in President Wilson's words, the AFC side of the Super Bowl was once again "safe for democracy." But this one was really no contest.

The Presidents claim victory in this match.

SUPER BOWL XXVIII

SCORE: Dallas Cowboys 30, Buffalo Bills 13 **DATE:** January 30, 1994
LOCATION: Georgia Dome, Atlanta, GA
REGULAR SEASON RECORDS: Cowboys 12–4, Bills 12–4
GAME MVP: Cowboys RB Emmitt Smith **TV AUDIENCE:** 90 million
COST OF 30-SECOND COMMERCIAL: $900,000

★ *Score After this Match* ★

PRESIDENTS	16
SUPER BOWLS	12
QUARTER	● ● ○ ●

HOME STATE: Ohio **PARTY:** Democratic
DATES AS PRESIDENT: 1921–1923
AGE AS PRESIDENT: 55 **REASON LEFT OFFICE:** Died in office
ELECTORAL VOTES: 1920: Harding 404, Cox 127

WARREN G. HARDING

In a 1962 survey of historians, *Warren G. Harding ranked thirty-first out of the 31 presidents who had served up to that time.*

By 1982, a Chicago Tribune poll placed Harding second to last, edging out William Henry Harrison, who died in office one month after his inauguration. That's like when the Cleveland Browns beat the Detroit Lions.

Harding himself spent only two and a half years on the job, also passing away while in office. He was a charismatic guy and a supporter of civil rights. But things didn't go really well under his watch. The Teapot Dome scandal remains a Superdome of political debacles, still half a page in many U.S. history books.

By 2009, in a C-SPAN survey, Harding had edged ahead of William Henry Harrison, Franklin Pierce, Andrew Johnson, and James Buchanan to rank as the thirty-eighth best president out of 42.

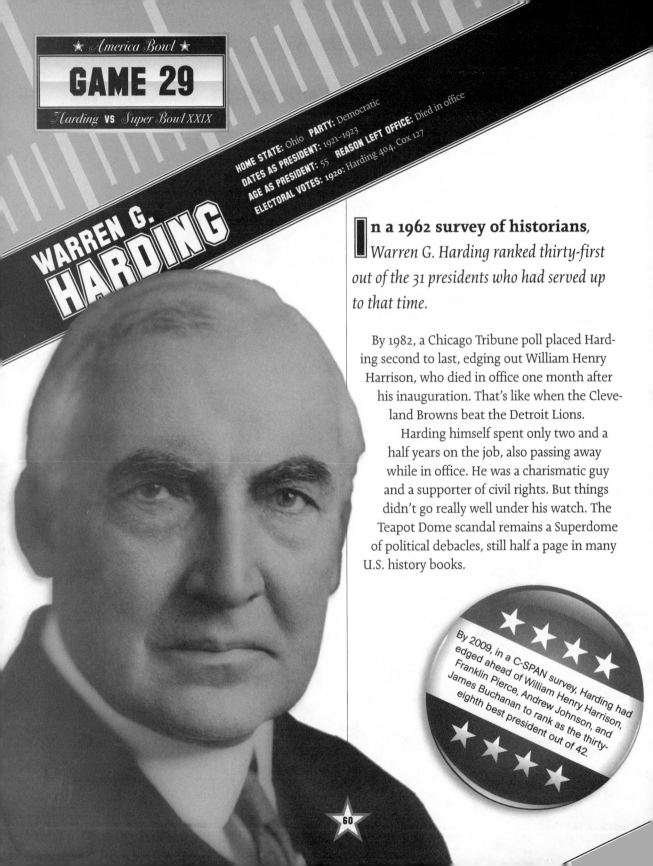

San Francisco 49ers
QB Steve Young

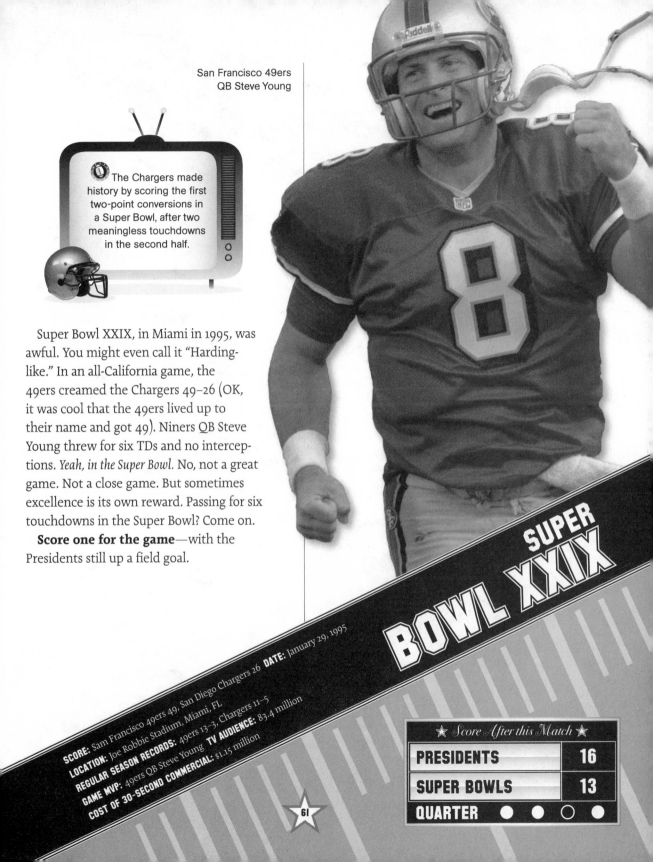

> The Chargers made history by scoring the first two-point conversions in a Super Bowl, after two meaningless touchdowns in the second half.

Super Bowl XXIX, in Miami in 1995, was awful. You might even call it "Harding-like." In an all-California game, the 49ers creamed the Chargers 49–26 (OK, it was cool that the 49ers lived up to their name and got 49). Niners QB Steve Young threw for six TDs and no interceptions. *Yeah, in the Super Bowl.* No, not a great game. Not a close game. But sometimes excellence is its own reward. Passing for six touchdowns in the Super Bowl? Come on.

Score one for the game—with the Presidents still up a field goal.

SUPER BOWL XXIX

SCORE: Sam Francisco 49ers 49, San Diego Chargers 26 **DATE:** January 29, 1995
LOCATION: Joe Robbie Stadium, Miami, FL
REGULAR SEASON RECORDS: 49ers 13–3, Chargers 11–5
GAME MVP: 49ers QB Steve Young **TV AUDIENCE:** 83.4 million
COST OF 30-SECOND COMMERCIAL: $1.15 million

★ *Score After this Match* ★

PRESIDENTS	16
SUPER BOWLS	13
QUARTER	● ● ○ ●

HOME STATE: Vermont **PARTY:** Republican
DATES AS PRESIDENT: 1923–1929
AGE AS PRESIDENT: 51 **REASON LEFT OFFICE:** Retired
ELECTORAL VOTES: 1924: Coolidge 382, Davis 136, La Folette 13

CALVIN COOLIDGE

There's a story, *a joke really, about thirtieth president Calvin Coolidge.*

Coolidge was famous, even while president, for not talking a lot. If this joke can be trusted, the great wit Dorothy Parker was at a White House dinner, and she said to him, "Mr. President, I made a bet with a friend that I can get more than two words out of you." He replied, "You lose." Pretty good line. Parker probably made it up. But Coolidge certainly kept things low-key while in office, and Miss Parker wasn't the only intellect to take note. H. L. Mencken wrote: "There were no thrills while he reigned, but neither were there any headaches. He had no ideas, and he was not a nuisance."

Teddy Roosevelt said, "Speak softly and carry a big stick." Calvin Coolidge just didn't speak much and was not big in the stick department. His nickname was "Silent Cal."

Here's what would have been a good line: if Cowboys cornerback Larry Brown pulled a Coolidge and said "you lose" to the Steelers during Super Bowl XXX. Brown rose from his own sort of quiet obscurity to pick off two Neil O'Donnell passes and help the Cowboys win 27–17.

The 1996 Super Bowl was a decent game. Not a classic. The Steelers never held the lead or even tied the game, but things kept threatening to become close. Pittsburgh got to within three points, trailing 20–17 in the fourth quarter, and then they sacked Cowboys QB Troy Aikman to force a punt and get the ball back late. But then the unheralded Larry Brown picked off a pass intended for backup WR Andre Hastings and took it to the Steelers' four-yard line. RB Emmitt Smith punched it in for the game-sealing TD. The Cowboys were on their way to being the "Team of the 1990s."

> Larry Brown would have just one more interception in his career after this Super Bowl. He retired after the 1998 season with 14 total regular-season interceptions.

Brown forever joined the list of "what's his name?" Super Bowl heroes who will always be remembered for stepping up big in the biggest game. (For example, remember that other guy, whatshisname?) Coolidge receded forever onto the list of presidents about whom not much more is remembered than their names. **Punch one in for the Super Bowls.**

SUPER BOWL XXX

SCORE: Dallas Cowboys 27, Pittsburgh Steelers 17 **DATE:** January 28, 1996
LOCATION: Sun Devil Stadium, Tempe, AZ
REGULAR SEASON RECORDS: Cowboys 12–4, Steelers 11–5
GAME MVP: Cowboys CB Larry Brown **TV AUDIENCE:** 94.08 million
COST OF 30-SECOND COMMERCIAL: $1.085 million

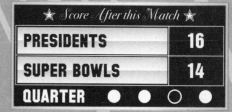

★ *Score After this Match* ★

PRESIDENTS	16
SUPER BOWLS	14
QUARTER	● ● ○ ●

HERBERT HOOVER

HOME STATE: Iowa **PARTY:** Republican
DATES AS PRESIDENT: 1929–1933
AGE AS PRESIDENT: 54 **REASON LEFT OFFICE:** Lost re-election
ELECTORAL VOTES: 1928: Hoover 444, Smith 87
1932: F.D. Roosevelt 472, Hoover 59

Hoover grew up poor but struck it rich as a businessman in the zinc mining industry. If only being president depended more on having expertise in zinc!

Here is a crossroads battle, a meeting of **two opponents heading in opposite directions.**

> I was the first president born west of the Mississippi River.

The once-great Green Bay Packers, entering Super Bowl XXXI in 1997, were resurgent. A generation had passed since the Packers had been in Super Bowl II in 1968. It had been a hard fall. But the Pack had the NFC's best regular-season record and blazed through the playoffs. Now they were on the road to glory again with the biggest prize in sight.

Herbert Hoover entered office in 1929 as the United States began its slide into the Great Depression. The stock market crashed in October.

Poorly regulated banks, and then other companies, failed. Soon a quarter of the country was unemployed. The nation spiraled into an abyss. Hoover, a self-made millionaire, did not seem capable of holding back the pain. He served one term and was done.

The Packers and Patriots played it close for a while. Pats QB Drew Bledsoe matched Packers QB Brett Favre in the first half, as they each tossed two TDs (Favre also ran for a TD to close the half). A New England touchdown toward the end of the third quarter pulled the Patriots within six points, at 27–21. Then the Packers ran away with

it—literally. Flashy returner Desmon Howard carried the ensuing kickoff 99 yards for a backbreaking touchdown: 35–21. That's how it ended. The Patriots' quest to "squeeze the cheese" had failed. Green Bay was riding high once more. Somewhere up there Coach Lombardi was smiling.

Score one for the Super Bowls.

> Patriots fans really did buy T-shirts with the slogan "Squeeze the Cheese" for the game against Green Bay.

> For their Super Bowl XX appearance against the Bears, Pats fans wore shirts that said "Berry the Bears," in honor of their coach Raymond Berry.

> Neither slogan worked.

Green Bay Packers QB Brett Favre drops back to make a pass

SUPER BOWL XXXI

SCORE: Green Bay Packers 35, New England Patriots 21 **DATE:** January 26, 1997
LOCATION: Louisiana Superdome, New Orleans, LA
REGULAR SEASON RECORDS: Packers 13–3, Patriots 11–5
GAME MVP: Packers kick returner (KR) Desmond Howard **TV AUDIENCE:** 87.87 million
COST OF 30-SECOND COMMERCIAL: $1.2 million

★ *Score After this Match* ★

PRESIDENTS	16
SUPER BOWLS	15
QUARTER	● ● ○ ●

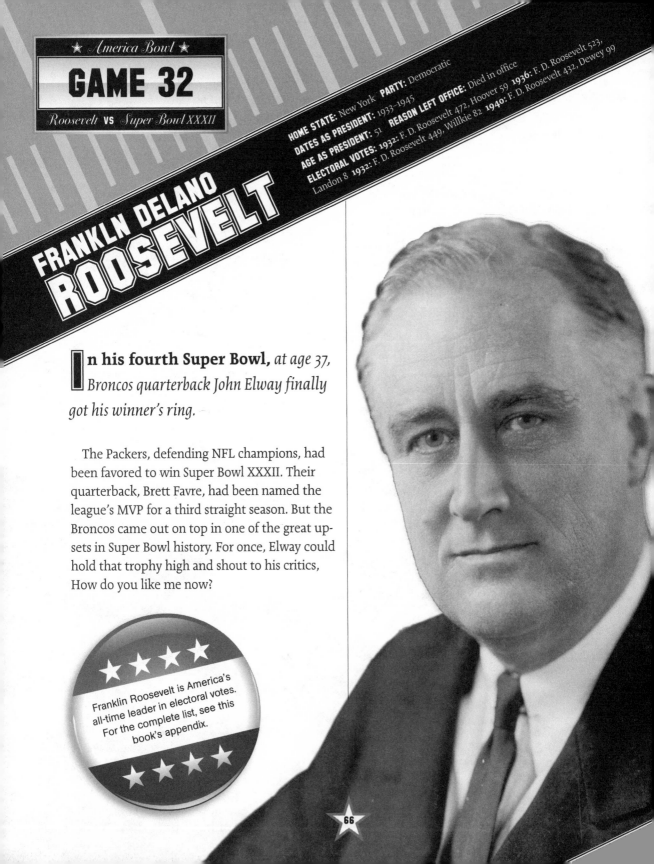

HOME STATE: New York **PARTY:** Democratic
DATES AS PRESIDENT: 1933–1945 **REASON LEFT OFFICE:** Died in office
AGE AS PRESIDENT: 51
ELECTORAL VOTES: 1932: F. D. Roosevelt 472, Hoover 59 **1936:** F. D. Roosevelt 523, Landon 8 **1932:** F. D. Roosevelt 449, Willkie 82 **1940:** F. D. Roosevelt 432, Dewey 99

FRANKLN DELANO ROOSEVELT

In his fourth Super Bowl, *at age 37, Broncos quarterback John Elway finally got his winner's ring.*

The Packers, defending NFL champions, had been favored to win Super Bowl XXXII. Their quarterback, Brett Favre, had been named the league's MVP for a third straight season. But the Broncos came out on top in one of the great upsets in Super Bowl history. For once, Elway could hold that trophy high and shout to his critics, How do you like me now?

Franklin Roosevelt is America's all-time leader in electoral votes. For the complete list, see this book's appendix.

It was close all the way through. Denver coach Mike Shanahan's blitz-happy defense swarmed Favre. Broncos RB Terrell Davis ran for three touchdowns, the last of them breaking a tie with 1:45 left in the game to make the final score Broncos 31, Packers 24. It was all you'd want in a game. Only for Packers fans was it a day that will live in infamy.

But sorry again, Mr. Elway. Now you must oppose Franklin Roosevelt, the greatest president of the twentieth century. Entering office while the Great Depression was ruining everything, FDR initiated New Deal reforms—the Works

Qualcomm Stadium also hosted the Yankees–Padres World Series in 1998—making it the only stadium in history to have the Super Bowl and World Series in the same year.

Terrell Davis has the NFL's second most career TDs for a player with the initials TD. Do you know who is number one?

Take a minute before reading the next sentence. Ready? It's Tony Dorsett.

Denver Broncos RB Terrell Davis

Progress Administration, Social Security—that helped get America back on its feet. Though confined to a wheelchair after being stricken with polio, FDR reminded America that "the only thing we have to fear is fear itself." He saw the country through World War II and a decisive beat-down of the Nazis. He was elected to four terms as president, a record that will never be broken. And under his administration, Prohibition was repealed—something all football fans can appreciate.

Yes, Elway punched his ticket to the Hall of Fame on January 25, 1998. But FDR isn't about to start losing now. With America Bowl getting tighter than ever, **score a clutch victory for the Presidents.**

SUPER BOWL XXXII

SCORE: Denver Broncos 31, Green Bay Packers 24 **DATE:** January 25, 1998
LOCATION: Qualcomm Stadium, San Diego, CA
REGULAR SEASON RECORDS: Broncos 12–4, Packers 13–3
GAME MVP: Broncos RB Terrell Davis **TV AUDIENCE:** 90 million
COST OF 30-SECOND COMMERCIAL: $1.3 million

★ *Score After this Match* ★

PRESIDENTS	17
SUPER BOWLS	15
QUARTER	● ● ○ ●

HOME STATE: Missouri **PARTY:** Democratic
DATES AS PRESIDENT: 1945–1953
AGE AS PRESIDENT: 60 **REASON LEFT OFFICE:** Did not seek re-election
ELECTORAL VOTES: 1948: Truman 303, Dewey 189, Thurmond 39

HARRY S. TRUMAN

Every master of sports trivia remembers Wally Pipp, the Yankees first baseman who sat out of the lineup for "one game" in 1925, only to be replaced by Lou Gehrig, who became known as the "Iron Man" by playing a then-record **2,130 consecutive games.**

Few remember the man who replaced Gehrig, though. It was Babe Dahlgren. (Boy, he had exactly the wrong nickname, too, didn't he?) Dahlgren played 12 unexceptional seasons for eight teams.

What does baseball trivia have to do with John Elway winning his second Super Bowl, or with thirty-third president Harry Truman? Well, Truman could have been the next Babe Dahlgren, stepping in as a relative nobody for the beloved Iron Man of presidents, Franklin Delano Roosevelt. Like Gehrig, FDR became ill after breaking the longevity record, among other Hall of Fame highlights. The fact that Truman made a name for himself working in such a long shadow says something—and sets us up for America Bowl Game 33.

The Broncos were supposed to win the big game this time, and they did. They beat the Falcons decisively, 34–19. There was a little bit of drama, some off the field. Atlanta coach Dan Reeves and Denver coach Mike Shanahan, former colleagues, made some mean pre-game statements. On the field, the Broncos picked off Falcons QB Chris Chandler three times. Elway passed for 336 yards, RB Terrell Davis ran for 102, and fullback Howard Griffith punched in two one-yard TDs.

Former midwestern senator Truman was a freshly minted vice president when he suddenly took the oath of office upon FDR's death. Many said, "Harry Who?" Few expected much from him, although it was a vital time with much to do. Truman was a plainspoken man of action. He dropped two atomic bombs on Japan in 1945 to savagely end that war, then chilled relations with the Soviet Union, pretty much starting the Cold War—also the Korean War. But his policies did help piece Europe back together after World War II. Domestically, his administration set up the GI Bill to help veterans thrive.

Historians rate Truman more kindly than contemporaries did. For Super Bowl XXXIII, there's not so much love, either then or now.

Score this one for the Presidents.

Denver Broncos
QB John Elway

Falcons coach Dan Reeves became the fourth head coach to lose four Super Bowls, joining an elite club that included Bud Grant, Don Shula, and Marv Levy. "Tough-luck" Reeves had lost his other Super Bowls coaching the Broncos!

Sorry, Dan, but this Super Bowl is mine!

SUPER BOWL XXXIII

SCORE: Denver Broncos 34, Atlanta Falcons 19 **DATE:** January 31, 1999
LOCATION: Pro Player Stadium, Miami, FL
REGULAR SEASON RECORDS: Broncos 14-2, Falcons 14-2
GAME MVP: Broncos QB John Elway **TV AUDIENCE:** 83.7 million
COST OF 30-SECOND COMMERCIAL: $1.6 million

★ *Score After this Match* ★

PRESIDENTS	18
SUPER BOWLS	15
QUARTER	● ● ● ○

HOME STATE: Texas **PARTY:** Republican
DATES AS PRESIDENT: 1953–1961
AGE AS PRESIDENT: 62 **REASON LEFT OFFICE:** Reached two-term limit
ELECTORAL VOTES: 1952: Eisenhower 442, Stevenson 89
1956: Eisenhower 457, Stevenson 73

DWIGHT D. EISENHOWER

H ey, we like Ike. He was the **president of the 1950s!**

The president of Elvis and Buddy Holly and Marilyn Monroe and the '57 Chevy. He took us from postwar gray to Happy Days. Got the space race rolling and the Interstate Highway System blasting off. The economy boomed. The suburbs

Eisenhower did have his own big finish. Although he was a career military man, his farewell address warned Americans to be on guard against the military-industrial complex, a growing alliance of big corporations and government military power. "The potential for the disastrous rise of misplaced power exists and will persist," he said. "We must never let the weight of this combination endanger our liberties or democratic processes."

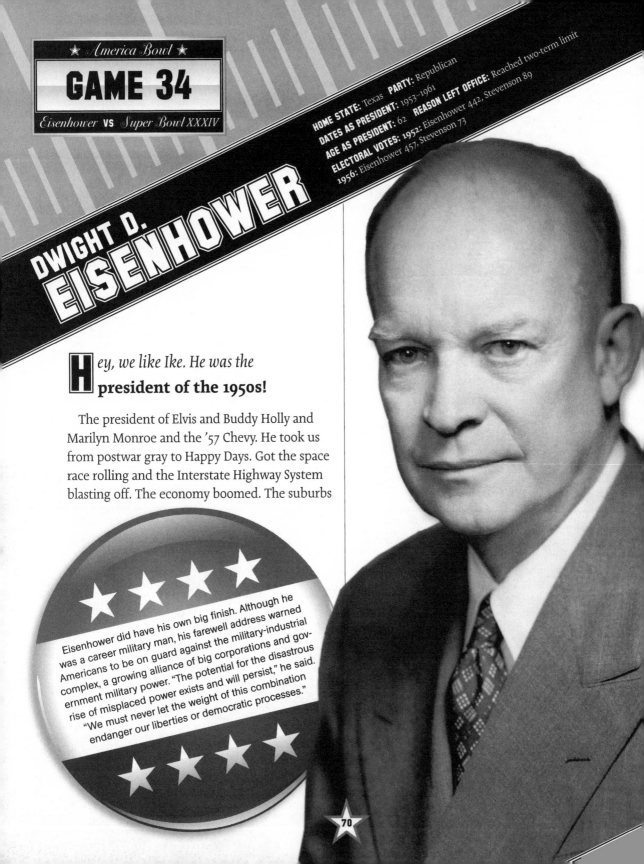

Three weeks before the Super Bowl, the Titans had won the love of the nation by pulling off an incredible play that came to be known as "the Music City Miracle."

Trailing by a point, the Titans received a kickoff with 16 seconds left. Lorenzo Neal handed the ball to TE Frank Wycheck, who lateraled it all the way across the field to WR Kevin Dyson.

Then Dyson ran it 75 yards for a game-winning touchdown.

sprawled. Adults dressed like adults. Men wore hats. Good times. Eisenhower probably would have gone for a third term if not for that pesky constitutional amendment.

Unfortunately, he was the thirty-fourth president, and Super Bowl XXXIV, in January 2000, was one of the best ever.

The Rams came in as a scoring machine, led by quick-chucking QB Kurt Warner and speedy WRs Torry Holt and Isaac Bruce—"the greatest show on turf." They jumped out to a 16–0 lead. But back came the Titans. QB Steve McNair threw and ran the ball downfield. RB Eddie George punched it in twice. Al Del Greco nailed a field goal with 2:12 left in the game to tie it at 16. On the Rams' first play with the ball back, Warner found Bruce at the Titans' 38-yard line, and Bruce took it home for a 73-yard TD play, putting the Rams ahead 23–16.

In a final drive, Tennessee got the ball at its own ten with 1:54 left. They drove downfield, and with time for just one more play, they had it at the Rams' ten. McNair hit WR Kevin Dyson with a quick pass, and Dyson made it to the two-yard line when Rams linebacker Mike Jones made what's now simply known as "the Tackle." He grabbed Dyson's legs and rolled,

as Dyson reached the ball as far as he could toward the plane of the goal line. The ball finished inches short of a score as the clock ran out.

And so, to start the fourth quarter of America Bowl, **a decade of newly exciting Super Bowl games begins.** Can the Presidents match the excitement and hold on to their lead? Get the popcorn—we're heading toward a thrilling finish.

SUPER BOWL XXXIV

SCORE: St. Louis Rams 23, Tennesse Titans 16 **DATE:** January 30, 2000
LOCATION: Georgia Dome, Atlanta, GA
REGULAR SEASON RECORDS: Rams 13–3, Titans 13–3
GAME MVP: Rams QB Kurt Warner **TV AUDIENCE:** 88.5 million
COST OF 30-SECOND COMMERCIAL: $1.1 million

★ Score After this Match ★

PRESIDENTS	18
SUPER BOWLS	16
QUARTER	● ● ● ○

HOME STATE: Massachusetts **PARTY:** Democratic
DATES AS PRESIDENT: 1961–1963
AGE AS PRESIDENT: 43 **REASON LEFT OFFICE:** Assassinated
ELECTORAL VOTES: 1960: Kennedy 303, Nixon 219

JOHN F. KENNEDY

How did John F. Kennedy beat Richard Nixon in the 1960 election? Some say it was because the two participated in the first U.S. presidential debate to be shown on TV. Kennedy just looked better on the little screen. The camera made it look like Nixon forgot to shave. Many people who listened to the debate on radio thought Nixon did great, but TV viewers had Kennedy winning easily. Pundits say politics changed forever after that.

Even years later, both the 2000–2001 Baltimore Ravens' season and John F. Kennedy's brief time in office have **left a bunch of unanswered questions.**

The Ravens weren't a perfect team. Dilfer was an average quarterback. Kennedy was neither a perfect man nor a perfect president. Somehow, both were able to make history.

The Ravens had the NFL's fourteenth best scoring offense during the regular season, hardly the credentials for a Super Bowl team. The quarterback who started their season, Tony Banks, threw eight interceptions in eight games and had a passer rating of 69. Dilfer took over after that and threw 11 interceptions in eight games, with a 76.6 rating. Like Kennedy, the Ravens had a tense October, losing three straight.

What the Ravens had, probably more so than Kennedy, was a strong defense, led by marauding linebacker Ray Lewis. They allowed the fewest points in the NFL. Entering the post-season as a wild card, they allowed just one touchdown in three playoff games, winning 21–3, 24–10, and 16–3. In Super Bowl XXXV the offense did what it needed to do, and the defense did what it always did. The Ravens trounced the Giants 34–7. They intercepted Giants QB Kerry Collins four times. Did someone once say the best way to win the big game is with big defense? It worked for the Ravens.

Kennedy was in office for just over two years before his assassination. He got in as a sort of wild card himself, with a family-funded campaign, some election-day chicanery, and a narrow margin of victory. Flaws? His Bay of Pigs attempt to overthrow Fidel Castro was a fiasco. The USSR's Nikita Kruschev got the better of him. The Berlin Wall must have seemed like a good idea at the time. He was a womanizing scoundrel. But JFK was young and telegenic and inspired the nation. He launched the Peace Corps and put muscle behind a space program that would plant a U.S. flag on the moon.

"The torch has passed to a new generation of Americans," he proclaimed. "Ask not what your country can do for you but what you can do for your country," he suggested. You know, stuff like that.

Apologies to Trent Dilfer and Ray Lewis, **but this victory goes to the Presidents.**

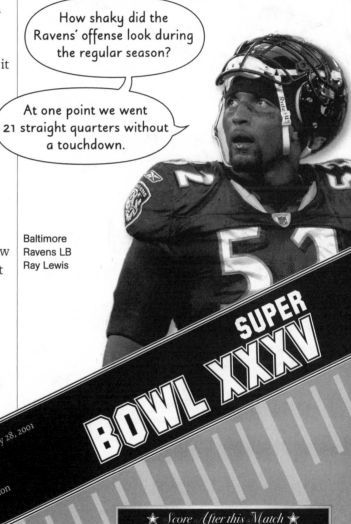

How shaky did the Ravens' offense look during the regular season?

At one point we went 21 straight quarters without a touchdown.

Baltimore Ravens LB Ray Lewis

SUPER BOWL XXXV

DATE: January 28, 2001
SCORE: Baltimore Ravens 34, New York Giants 7
LOCATION: Raymond James Stadium, Tampa, FL
REGULAR SEASON RECORDS: Ravens 12–4, Giants 12–4
GAME MVP: Ravens LB Ray Lewis
TV AUDIENCE: 84.3 million
COST OF 30-SECOND COMMERCIAL: $2.1 million

★ Score After this Match ★	
PRESIDENTS	19
SUPER BOWLS	16
QUARTER	● ● ● ○

HOME STATE: Texas
PARTY: Democratic
DATES AS PRESIDENT: 1963–1969
AGE AS PRESIDENT: 55
REASON LEFT OFFICE: Did not see re-election
ELECTORAL VOTES: 1964: Johnson 486, Goldwater 52

LYNDON B. JOHNSON

In 1968, NASA successfully launched Apollo 8, the first manned spaceflight to escape the gravitational field of Earth. It entered the gravity of the moon and returned safely.

Here is a story *of two eager backups thrust by emergency into number one roles under less than ideal circumstances.*

Lyndon Johnson, who'd never enjoyed being vice president to John F. Kennedy, was rushed to Dallas and sworn in as the thirty-sixth president after Kennedy was shot on November 22, 1963. Novice QB Tom Brady, who'd played in only one NFL game in his career, stepped in as the Patriots' starting quarterback after Drew Bledsoe went down with an injury in week 2 of the 2001 season—a season that also was scarred by the tragedy of 9/11 off the field.

Johnson had great moments, but he was a one-way player. Domestically he was first-string, maybe a Hall of Fame candidate. His tenure from 1963 to 1969—which included a landslide election win in 1964—saw passage of landmark legislation, including the Civil Rights Act of 1964 outlawing racial discrimination, the Voting Rights Act of 1965 banning racist polling rules, and the Public Broadcasting Act of 1967 creating public TV and radio. He launched Medicare, Medicaid, Food Stamps, Head Start, environmental protection laws, and the National Endowments for the Arts and the Humanities. Foreign policy was the hole in his game, though. He hated having to devote time and resources to the war in Vietnam. But he refused to lose and increased rather than drew down U.S. involvement. Ultimately it was his frustration with ceaseless war issues, at home and abroad, that led LBJ to choose not to run in 1968.

Tom Brady came up huge in the Patriots' emotional 2001 season, which was played in the dark shadow of the 9/11 attacks. With the poise of a veteran, Brady led New England to an unlikely division title. He seemed charmed. The Pats got a

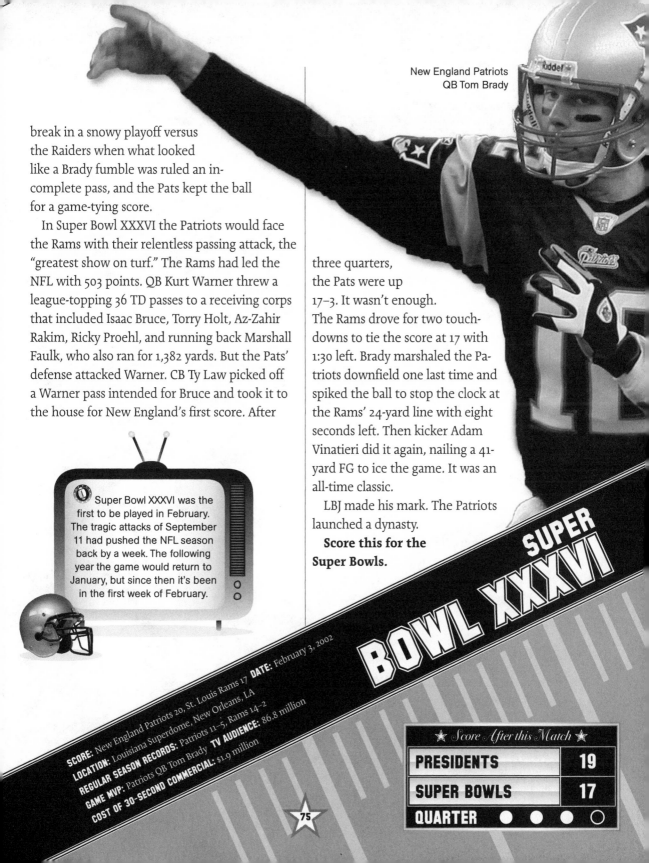

New England Patriots
QB Tom Brady

break in a snowy playoff versus the Raiders when what looked like a Brady fumble was ruled an incomplete pass, and the Pats kept the ball for a game-tying score.

In Super Bowl XXXVI the Patriots would face the Rams with their relentless passing attack, the "greatest show on turf." The Rams had led the NFL with 503 points. QB Kurt Warner threw a league-topping 36 TD passes to a receiving corps that included Isaac Bruce, Torry Holt, Az-Zahir Rakim, Ricky Proehl, and running back Marshall Faulk, who also ran for 1,382 yards. But the Pats' defense attacked Warner. CB Ty Law picked off a Warner pass intended for Bruce and took it to the house for New England's first score. After

three quarters, the Pats were up 17–3. It wasn't enough. The Rams drove for two touchdowns to tie the score at 17 with 1:30 left. Brady marshaled the Patriots downfield one last time and spiked the ball to stop the clock at the Rams' 24-yard line with eight seconds left. Then kicker Adam Vinatieri did it again, nailing a 41-yard FG to ice the game. It was an all-time classic.

LBJ made his mark. The Patriots launched a dynasty.

Score this for the Super Bowls.

Super Bowl XXXVI was the first to be played in February. The tragic attacks of September 11 had pushed the NFL season back by a week. The following year the game would return to January, but since then it's been in the first week of February.

SUPER BOWL XXXVI

SCORE: New England Patriots 20, St. Louis Rams 17 **DATE:** February 3, 2002
LOCATION: Louisiana Superdome, New Orleans, LA
REGULAR SEASON RECORDS: Patriots 11–5, Rams 14–2
GAME MVP: Patriots QB Tom Brady **TV AUDIENCE:** 86.8 million
COST OF 30-SECOND COMMERCIAL: $1.9 million

★ Score After this Match ★

PRESIDENTS	19
SUPER BOWLS	17
QUARTER	● ● ● ○

RICHARD M. NIXON

HOME STATE: California **PARTY:** Republican
DATES AS PRESIDENT: 1969–1974
AGE AS PRESIDENT: 56 **REASON LEFT OFFICE:** Resigned
ELECTORAL VOTES: 1960: Kennedy 303, Nixon 219 **1968:** Nixon 301, Humphrey 191, Wallace 46
1972: Nixon 520, McGovern 17

Ask yourself this. *Which of these two statements is more unbelievable: "Richard Nixon has resigned from the presidency in disgrace" or "Ladies and gentlemen, your Super Bowl champions: the Tampa Bay Buccaneers"?*

The Bucs had become a benchmark for badness in the NFL. They started in the league in 1976 and lost their first 26 games. Going into the 2002 season, they had compiled exactly twice as

In 1974, Richard Nixon became the only president to resign while in office. He made no further comebacks.

many losses as wins: 131–262–1. But new coach Jon Gruden took them all the way this season, crushing the favored Raiders 48–21. The tenacious Tampa defense picked off Raiders QB Rich Gannon five times. Suddenly, we didn't have Tampa Bay to kick around anymore.

Unlike Gruden, Nixon's ambition to come out on top got the better of him. His political comeback, after he'd lost the election of 1960, was gutsy. But he trusted no one. He made lists of enemies. The cover-up of the 1972 Watergate break-in eventually pointed to him, and he was done. In the end, his strengths and weaknesses meant little compared to his legacy: leaving a generation of Americans distrustful of their government.

And so Nixon is done here, too. Super Bowl XXVII wasn't filled with offensive fireworks. The Buccaneers became the first team in Super Bowl history to score three defensive touchdowns. But there were no major scandals in the game (although Gruden had previously

Super Bowl XXXVII was the first Super Bowl to feature two teams named after pirates.

coached the Raiders and knew their plays). Nobody resigned in dishonor (however, Raiders lineman Barret Robbins did go missing from the team in the days before the game, ended up in a hospital for depression, and did not play). **The Presidents drop another key game.** The Super Bowls are knocking on the door.

SUPER BOWL XXXVII

SCORE: Tampa Bay Buccaneers 48, Oakland Raiders 21 **DATE:** January 26, 2003
LOCATION: Qualcomm Stadium, San Diego, CA
REGULAR SEASON RECORDS: Buccaneers 12–4, Raiders 11–5
GAME MVP: Buccaneers S Dexter Jackson **TV AUDIENCE:** 88.6 million
COST OF 30-SECOND COMMERCIAL: $2.1 million

★ Score After this Match ★	
PRESIDENTS	19
SUPER BOWLS	18
QUARTER	● ● ● ○

77

HOME STATE: Nebraska **PARTY:** Republican
DATES AS PRESIDENT: 1974–1977
AGE AS PRESIDENT: 61 **REASON LEFT OFFICE:** Lost re-election
ELECTORAL VOTES: 1976: Carter 297, Ford 240

GERALD R. FORD

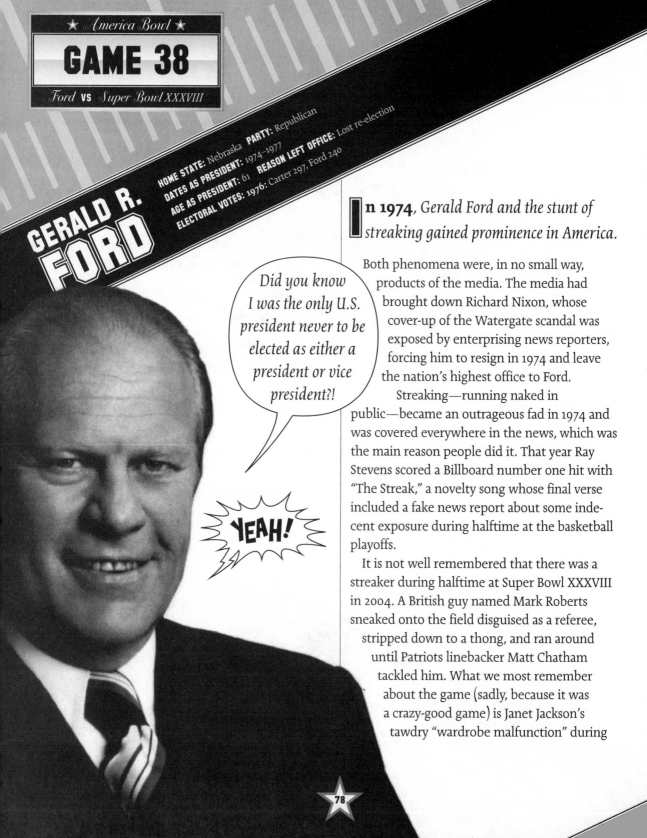

Did you know I was the only U.S. president never to be elected as either a president or vice president?!

YEAH!

In 1974, *Gerald Ford and the stunt of streaking gained prominence in America.*

Both phenomena were, in no small way, products of the media. The media had brought down Richard Nixon, whose cover-up of the Watergate scandal was exposed by enterprising news reporters, forcing him to resign in 1974 and leave the nation's highest office to Ford.

Streaking—running naked in public—became an outrageous fad in 1974 and was covered everywhere in the news, which was the main reason people did it. That year Ray Stevens scored a Billboard number one hit with "The Streak," a novelty song whose final verse included a fake news report about some indecent exposure during halftime at the basketball playoffs.

It is not well remembered that there was a streaker during halftime at Super Bowl XXXVIII in 2004. A British guy named Mark Roberts sneaked onto the field disguised as a referee, stripped down to a thong, and ran around until Patriots linebacker Matt Chatham tackled him. What we most remember about the game (sadly, because it was a crazy-good game) is Janet Jackson's tawdry "wardrobe malfunction" during

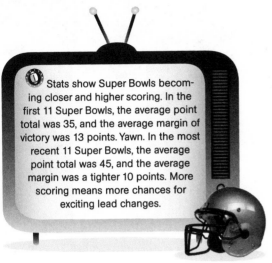
Overtime? No, sir. Brady led the Pats inside Carolina's 30, and Adam Vinatieri kicked a 41-yard field goal to win the game as time ran out.

Ford, himself a former football player, stands no chance of matching this classic. He pardoned Nixon and signed the Helsinki Accords to thaw the Cold War a bit. He lost his job to Jimmy Carter, who comes up next in America Bowl. Can you feel the momentum turning? **The Super Bowls tie up the score.**

Super Bowl MVP and New England Patriots QB Tom Brady

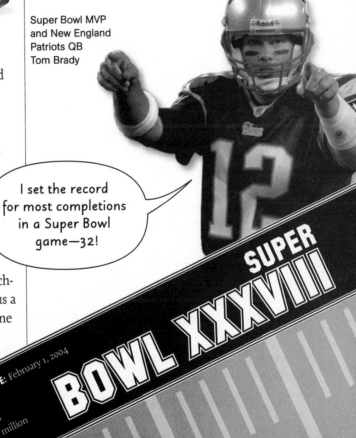

the official halftime show. Mr. Roberts' run in the buff came after Jackson's act. What a bad day to streak! Next to Jackson's choreographed display, his act seemed even more rinky-dink than it was already.

Super Bowl XXXVIII was tremendous entertainment. Back and forth it went. The Patriots scored, then the Panthers . . . then Patriots, Panthers, Patriots, Panthers. The fourth quarter was unbelievable, with 37 points scored. QB Jake Delhomme led the Panthers to two TDs to take a 22–21 lead with 6:53 on the clock. New England got the ball back and drove 68 yards for a touchdown—a Tom Brady pass to Mike Vrabel—plus a two-point conversion: Patriots 29–22. With time ticking down, the Panthers punched back. Delhomme capped a drive with a TD pass to WR Ricky Proehl, making it 29–29 with 1:08 to play.

I set the record for most completions in a Super Bowl game—32!

SUPER BOWL XXXVIII

SCORE: New England Patriots 32, Carolina Panthers 29 **DATE:** February 1, 2004

LOCATION: Reliant Stadium, Houston, TX

REGULAR SEASON RECORDS: Patriots 14–2, Panthers 11–5

GAME MVP: Patriots QB Tom Brady **TV AUDIENCE:** 89.8 million

COST OF 30-SECOND COMMERCIAL: $2.2 million

★ *Score After this Match* ★

PRESIDENTS	19
SUPER BOWLS	19
QUARTER	● ● ● ○

Many cartoons depicted Jimmy Carter with a smiling face on the body of a peanut.

JIMMY CARTER

HOME STATE: Georgia **PARTY:** Democratic
DATES AS PRESIDENT: 1977–1981
AGE AS PRESIDENT: 52 **REASON LEFT OFFICE:** Lost re-election
ELECTORAL VOTES: 1976: Carter 297, Ford 240, Reagan 1
1980: Reagan 489, Carter 49

Patriots versus Eagles. **Talk about an "America Bowl."**

This game threatened to break out into excitement on several occasions, and it stayed close all the way. By beating the Eagles in Super Bowl XXXIX, Pats QB Tom Brady lifted his career record to 3–0 in Super Bowls and 9–0 in the post-season. Basically he was making a mockery of the NFL's "Any Given Sunday" mantra—the idea that any team can beat any other team if they really want it. On the contrary, it seemed like the more a game mattered, the more invulnerable Brady and his Patriots had become.

Philly scored first, and Eagles receiver Terrell Owens, coming back from a broken leg, was stunning with nine catches for 122 yards. But by the end of the second quarter, Brady had his rhythm. He hit receiver Deion Branch to spearhead touchdown drives late in the second quarter and early in the third. Pats RB Corey Dillon started finding holes; his runs allowed Brady to use play-action passes to keep it moving. With the score tied at 14–14, Brady rattled off a quick flare to Troy Brown and a dropped dump pass out of the shotgun to RB Kevin Faulk. Then in a beautiful play-action, Brady faked a hand-off to Branch, and Branch sprinted to the sideline to haul in a pass. Five plays later, Dillon punched in another TD, and the Patriots were up 21–14 (and a FG made it 24–14).

My full name is James Earl Carter Jr., but (because I'm friendly!) I took the official oath of office as "Jimmy."

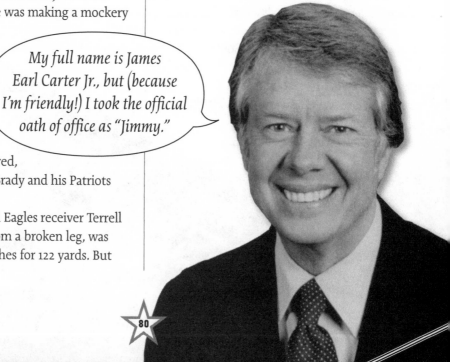

The Eagles had a little time to come back—but acted like they had a lot. With 5:40 left, they took almost four minutes to drive downfield and make it 24–21. When a Patriots punt gave the Eagles the ball at their own four, the only thing QB Donovan McNabb had time for was to chuck a game-ending interception. Philly fans ever since have doubted coach Andy Reid's clock-management expertise and McNabb's stamina (allegedly he was nauseous and exhausted during the final scoring drive).

Jimmy Carter came into office amid high hopes and tough times. The former peanut farmer and naval officer from Georgia found it difficult to get traction during a period of inflation, recession, disco, and general national crankiness in the late 1970s. His affable personality magnified the sense that maybe he was just too wimpy to get it done. It's unclear whether anyone got nauseous, but it didn't end well. It was in November 1979 that 52 Americans were

Several NFL greats appeared in the 1999 football movie *Any Given Sunday*, including Johnny Unitas, Warren Moon, and Jim Brown (shown below).

taken hostage in Iran and held for 14 months, a period that included the presidential election of 1980, in which Carter got the goobers beaten out of him by Ronald Reagan.

Carter, make no mistake, was a genuine patriot. **But he was no Super Bowl XXXIX.**

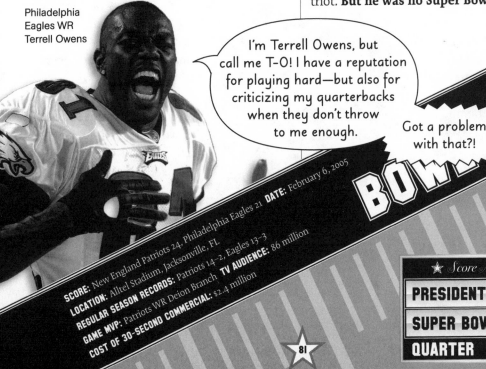

Philadelphia Eagles WR Terrell Owens

I'm Terrell Owens, but call me T-O! I have a reputation for playing hard—but also for criticizing my quarterbacks when they don't throw to me enough.

Got a problem with that?!

SUPER BOWL XXXIX

SCORE: New England Patriots 24, Philadelphia Eagles 21 **DATE:** February 6, 2005
LOCATION: Alltel Stadium, Jacksonville, FL
REGULAR SEASON RECORDS: Patriots 14-2, Eagles 13-3
GAME MVP: Patriots WR Deion Branch **TV AUDIENCE:** 86 million
COST OF 30-SECOND COMMERCIAL: $2.4 million

★ *Score After this Match* ★

PRESIDENTS	19
SUPER BOWLS	20
QUARTER	● ● ● ○

HOME STATE: Illinois **PARTY:** Republican
DATES AS PRESIDENT: 1981–1989
AGE AS PRESIDENT: 69 **REASON LEFT OFFICE:** Reached two-term limit
ELECTORAL VOTES: 1980: Reagan 483, Carter 49, Anderson 0
1984: Reagan 525, Mondale 13

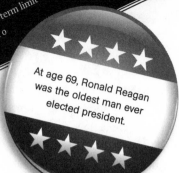

At age 69, Ronald Reagan was the oldest man ever elected president.

RONALD REAGAN

Super Bowl XL in 2005 was blanketed in **feel-good symbolism,** *but on the field was an error-plagued dud.*

Ronald Reagan came in with a similar approach as the fortieth U.S. president—but he made it work.

The Steelers were back in the Super Bowl after a ten-year absence, trying again to win their fifth Super Bowl ring—or "One for the Thumb," as the braggy rallying cry went.

This game would be the final stop for "The Bus," 13-year-veteran running back Jerome Bettis, who'd never won a Super Bowl. The Steelers began the season poorly and were seeded sixth in the AFC playoffs, then they made a storybook surge to reach the Super Bowl. The Seahawks, led by QB Matt Hasselbeck and RB Shaun Alexander, had an NFC-leading 13–3 record but still came in as underdogs.

Pittsburgh's 21–10 win was messy and controversial. Steelers QB Ben Roethlisberger, in becoming the youngest QB to win a Super Bowl, threw for just 123 yards, no touchdowns, and two interceptions—for a rating of 22.6.

Really? Besides his 75-yard TD scamper, Steelers RB Willie Parker racked up 18 yards. Bettis, the team's goal-line pile-driver, didn't see the end zone. The Seahawks were plagued by dropped passes and so many drive-killing penalties that coach Mike Holmgren probably still has nightmares.

Reagan rode in promising a hopeful new "morning in America." For the most part, he delivered. The economy and the national mood lifted during his two terms from 1981 to 1988. Some wondered whether the former actor was up to the task. He sure did like to simplify stuff. He said: "All the waste in a year from a nuclear power plant can be stored under a desk." His idea for a space-based "Star Wars" defense against Soviet missiles seemed outlandish. But it may have helped negotiations with Soviet leader Mikhail Gorbachev that led to a scaling back of nuclear arms. Ultimately, unable to hold together, the USSR dissolved. Reagan ran up a huge deficit and let corporations run wild in a "greed is good" era of leveraged buyouts, big-hair bands, and shoulder pads. He let underlings carry out the illegal shenanigans of the Iran-Contra scandal.

But Reagan remains an icon of American swagger and self-sufficiency. **And so "The Gipper" wins one for the Presidents**, who end a four-game losing streak and even the score as America Bowl's clock ticks down.

Pittsburgh Steelers
WR Hines Ward

This would be another chance to win a Super Bowl for Steelers head coach Bill Cowher, who'd been at the helm since 1992 but lost in his only previous trip to the big game, 27–17 to the Cowboys in Super Bowl XXX. He got his ring this time.

FINALLY!

SUPER BOWL XL

SCORE: Pittsburgh Steelers 21, Seattle Seahawks 10 **DATE:** February 5, 2006
LOCATION: Ford Field, Detroit, MI
REGULAR SEASON RECORDS: Steelers 11–5, Seahawks 13–3
GAME MVP: Steelers WR Hines Ward **TV AUDIENCE:** 90.7 million
COST OF 30-SECOND COMMERCIAL: $2.5 million

★ Score After this Match ★	
PRESIDENTS	20
SUPER BOWLS	20
QUARTER ● ● ● ○	

GAME 41

Bush **VS** *Super Bowl XLI*

GEORGE H. W. BUSH

HOME STATE: Massachusetts **PARTY:** Republican

DATES AS PRESIDENT: 1989–1993

AGE AS PRESIDENT: 65 **REASON LEFT OFFICE:** Lost re-election

ELECTORAL VOTES: 1988: Bush 426, Dukakis 111

1992: Clinton 370, Bush 168, Perot 0

We don't have royal families *in American government or football.*

Here's about as close as it gets. Prescott Bush was a Wall Street banking tycoon from Connecticut who became a U.S. senator in 1952. He never made it to president, but he had a son and a grandson who did. Archie Manning was a quarterback for the New Orleans Saints from 1972 to 1982. He never made it to the Super Bowl, but he had two sons who did. Family connections don't guarantee a ride to the top in the NFL or the USA, but these guys show it sure doesn't hurt.

Archie's sons Peyton Manning and Eli Manning both won Super Bowls. Peyton entered rain-soaked Super Bowl XLI in 2007 respected

Operation Desert Storm, America's first Gulf War, popularized the idea of the government publicly giving nicknames to wars and battles, similar to the way boxing promoter Don King started labeling championship fights years earlier with names such as "the Rumble in the Jungle" and "the Thrilla in Manila."

as a great quarterback but with a reputation for not winning the big ones. And it didn't look good this time, either, when Chicago Bears return specialist Devin Hester took the game's opening kickoff back 93 yards for a score—the first TD on an opening kickoff in Super Bowl history. Later that quarter, a Thomas Jones run set up a Rex Grossman–to–Muhsin Muhammad TD pass that gave the Bears a 14–6 lead after one quarter.

But Manning and the Colts' defense pushed back. By the half, the Colts were up 16–14. They then turned to a ball-control offense, setting loose RBs Dominic Rhodes and Joseph Addai to eat time. They combined for 190 ground yards. The Colts' defense, spearheaded by safety Bob Sanders, forced three Bears fumbles in the game and intercepted Grossman twice in the fourth quarter to seal a 29–17 win. When it was done, Tony Dungy was the first African American head coach to win a Super Bowl.

George Herbert Walker Bush sailed into office as Ronald Reagan's longtime VP. His international expertise as former director of the CIA, and his connections to big business and the oil industry, seemed to color some of his key moves. The Berlin Wall came down under Bush's watch. When Iraq invaded oil-rich Kuwait, Bush launched Operation Desert Storm to push Iraq out—and begin a new era of U.S. involvement in the Persian Gulf. Domestically, he did not control the ball. He said, "Read my lips. No new

Besides the Mannings, other notable NFL father–son legacies include Phil and Chris Simms, Kellen Winslow I and II, Joe and Dan Klecko, and Mosi and Lofa Tatupu.

taxes!" but there were more taxes. The government paid a king's ransom to failed, poorly regulated savings and loans. By 1992, the economy was hurting super badly, and Bush lost his seat to Bill Clinton.

Score this for the Super Bowls. They go one point up as we head into the thrilling final weekend of America Bowl. Consider this our own version of the two-minute warning.

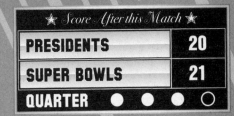

SUPER BOWL XLI

SCORE: Indianapolis Colts 29, Chicago Bears 17 **DATE:** February 4, 2007
LOCATION: Dolphin Stadium, Miami, FL
REGULAR SEASON RECORDS: Colts 12–4, Bears 13–3
GAME MVP: Colts QB Peyton Manning **TV AUDIENCE:** 93.2 million
COST OF 30-SECOND COMMERCIAL: $2.6 million

★ *Score After this Match* ★

PRESIDENTS	20
SUPER BOWLS	21
QUARTER	● ● ● ○

WILLIAM JEFFERSON CLINTON

HOME STATE: Arkansas **PARTY:** Democratic
DATES AS PRESIDENT: 1993–2001
AGE AS PRESIDENT: 46 **REASON LEFT OFFICE:** Reached two-term limit
ELECTORAL VOTES: 1993: Clinton 370, Bush 168
1996: Clinton 379, Dole 159

Perfection is an **unforgiving master.**

The New England Patriots entered Super Bowl XLII with an 18–0 record, on the cusp of recording the only 19–0 season in NFL history. Souvenir T-shirts proclaiming "19–0" were printed. All New England needed to do was defeat the underdog New York Giants, a team the Patriots had already beaten during the season. Bill Clinton, from as early as high school, groomed himself to become the perfect politician. He was brilliant and studied hard. He was handsome and skilled at winning people over. All the pieces were in place. Here's what happened.

Clinton entered the White House in 1993 amid a down economy, but soon was presiding over a long stretch of relative peace and great prosperity. The explosion of the Internet and the stock market boom created millionaires everywhere, invigorated America's entrepreneurial spirit, and changed lifestyles. Jobs were up, crime was down, music was free. Life seemed easy. But Clinton had an Achilles heel. Even before he won the presidency, news of extramarital affairs had begun to emerge, and it would only get worse, giving ammunition to his political opponents. In 1995, he had an improper relationship with White House intern Monica Lewinsky, and his denials led the House of Representatives to impeach him in 1998 (he remained in office). It was a disgrace that would forever taint his standing in history. By the time Clinton's vice president Al Gore ran for president in 2000, Gore didn't even use Clinton's name to help him.

The Patriots didn't undo themselves. It took perhaps the greatest play in Super Bowl history to threaten the Patriots' perfection. The game had been a tough defensive battle for three quarters, and the final frame began with the

> *Did you know the Internet bubble coincided with my presidency and ended just after my tenure?*

> At ESPN's 2008 ESPY Awards, they showed a fake behind-the-scenes film in which host Justin Timberlake,

> standing on the Giants' sideline during Super Bowl XLII,

> put a sticky wad of chewed gum on Tyree's helmet before the big play, explaining: "Who cares, man? This guy never plays anyway."

Patriots up 7–3. The lead would change hands a few more times. Giants QB Eli Manning led an 80-yard drive, which included a 45-yard pass to rookie TE Kevin Boss and ended on a TD pass to WR David Tyree to put the Giants up 10–7 with 11:05 left. After some back and forth, Tom Brady and the Pats drove back with a clock-munching drive. Brady found Randy Moss in the end zone to regain the lead, 14–10.

The Giants had about two minutes to make history. On a key third-and-five from his own 44 with 1:15 left, Manning dropped back and soon found three Patriots reaching over Giants blockers to grab his jersey, clutching at his number 10 from behind. Somehow he twisted out of their grasp, ran back a few yards into a safe spot, and looked desperately for a receiver. He chucked the ball downfield toward Tyree, who raised both hands and brought the ball down on top of his helmet. Are you kidding me? Tyree pressed the ball tight against his head and held on for his life as Patriots safety Rodney Harrison leveled him. The only thing more incredible than Manning's scramble was the ridiculous catch. Four plays later, Manning found WR Plaxico Burress in the corner of the end zone to give the Giants a breathtaking 17–14 win.

Yes, perfection is tough.

That's why they call it perfection. Despite his flaws, Clinton had a good run. But he didn't have the helmet catch. **This match goes to the Super Bowls, now up by two points in America Bowl with two matches left.** George Bush and Barack Obama are the Presidents' last hope—can they do it? Take your protein pill and put your helmet on—here comes the season finale.

SCORE: New York Giants 17, New England Patriots 14 **DATE:** February 3, 2008
LOCATION: University of Phoenix Stadium, Glendale, AZ
REGULAR SEASON RECORDS: Patriots 16–0, Giants 10–6
GAME MVP: Giants QB Eli Manning **TV AUDIENCE:** 97.5 million
COST OF 30-SECOND COMMERCIAL: $2.7 million

SUPER BOWL XLII

★ *Score After this Match* ★

PRESIDENTS	**20**
SUPER BOWLS	**22**
QUARTER	● ● ● ○

GEORGE W. BUSH

HOME STATE: Connecticut **PARTY:** Republican
DATES AS PRESIDENT: 2001–2009
AGE AS PRESIDENT: 54 **REASON LEFT OFFICE:** Reached two-term limit
ELECTORAL VOTES: 2000: G. W. Bush 271, Gore 266
2004: G. W. Bush 286, Kerry 252

George Bush became known for his verbal fumblings, and several humor books of "Bush-isms" were published during his two terms in office. He once said someone "misunder-estimated" him, and he told America "you're working hard to put food on your family."

This is a must-win *match for the Presidents here in America Bowl.*

They're down by two points, with two matches to go. There are no timeouts left. There is no margin for error. Here comes George W. Bush.

Bush, son of forty-first president George H. W. Bush, came into office by squeezing past Al Gore in the disputed election of 2000. Bush got some tough breaks and found it hard to get a rhythm going. The Internet bubble burst, the stock market plummeted, and it turned out that Texas energy giant Enron was a sham. Terrorists struck America on September 11, 2001. Terrorist leader Osama Bin Laden escaped U.S. forces in Afghanistan. The United States invaded Iraq to stop "weapons of mass destruction," which were never found. "Mission Accomplished" was declared in the Iraq invasion, and Iraqi leader Saddam Hussein was brought to justice, but bombings and chaos continued. Photos were released of U.S. soldiers torturing prisoners at

Abu Ghraib. Hurricane Katrina did not go well. The federal deficit reached an all-time record. Bush left office with low approval ratings, but the nation at least hadn't experienced another terrorist attack after 9/11 during his administration.

Super Bowl XLIII started slowly, then just kept getting better. Early on, it was all Steelers, going for their sixth ring. Just when the Arizona Cardinals, down 10–7, were about to drive it into the Steelers' end zone late in the first half, Steelers LB James Harrison picked off a Kurt Warner pass and ran it back 100 yards for the longest TD in Super Bowl history. Pittsburgh added

a FG in the low-scoring third quarter to make it 20–7. Six-burgh!

No team in Super Bowl history had come back from a 13-point deficit to win. But in the fourth quarter, Cardinals star WR Larry Fitzgerald made a leaping end-zone grab to make it 20–14. A Steelers' holding penalty in their own end zone caused a safety: 20–16. Then Warner hit Fitzgerald streaking at midfield on a post pattern for a 64-yard TD, incredibly, to put Arizona up 23–20 with 2:37 left.

QB Ben Roethlisberger drove the Steelers back into the Cardinals' red zone. With 49 seconds and no timeouts left, he fired a laser pass deep to the left corner of the Cardinals' end zone—it whizzed past the fingers of WR Santonio Holmes. On the next play, the Steelers tried the same thing in the right-side corner. Holmes stretched and held on to the ball as he dragged his toes to stay in bounds. Steelers win!

On the sidelines as confetti fell, Roethlisberger was handed a cell phone. It was Barack Obama, the new president, congratulating him on the victory. Obama didn't know it at the time, but he was also conceding the Presidents' defeat in America Bowl. **The Presidents lose this round,** and Super Bowl XLIV vs. Obama, coming up next, could be a good one, but it will be played only for pride.

> Their win in Super Bowl XLIII gave the Steelers six Super Bowl rings, putting them one ahead of the 49ers and Cowboys to lead the all-time list.

> I, James Harrison, am just one of the Super Bowl stars to share the name of a president.

> Check out this book's appendix for more!

Pittsburgh Steelers
LB James Harrison

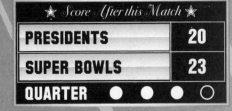

SUPER BOWL XLIII

SCORE: Pittsburgh Steelers 27, Arizona Cardinals 23 DATE: February 1, 2009
LOCATION: Raymond James Stadium, Tampa, FL
REGULAR SEASON RECORDS: Steelers 12–4, Cardinals 9–7
GAME MVP: Steelers WR Santonio Holmes, TV AUDIENCE: 98.7 million
COST OF 30-SECOND COMMERCIAL: $3 million

★ Score After this Match ★

PRESIDENTS	20
SUPER BOWLS	23
QUARTER	● ● ● ○

HOME STATE: Hawaii PARTY: Democratic
DATES AS PRESIDENT: 2010–
AGE AS PRESIDENT: 47
ELECTORAL VOTES: 2008: Obama 365, McCain 173

Barack Obama had a quick rise in politics. He became a U.S. senator in January 2005 and announced his candidacy for president about two years later in February 2007.

BARACK OBAMA

Going into Super Bowl XLIV, **there was some debate** *about how this match was going to work.*

Would we compare Barack Obama against the whole game, or only its first quarter? After all, Obama had just reached the first year, the first quarter of his four-year term. Was it fair to judge him against a Super Bowl that played out to the end, so everyone knows how it turned out?

Well, yes. That's what a Super Bowl is. Four quarters of football. If you'd judged Super Bowl XLIV by its first quarter, it would have been too early: the Colts won the quarter, 10–0, the Saints couldn't get a thing done against an unbending Indianapolis defense, and the game didn't seem exciting or surprising at all.

In the second quarter, the Saints started to find their groove. They ran 26 offensive plays, compared to six for the Colts. They couldn't reach the end zone yet, but kicker Garrett Hartley

drilled two field goals, and the New Orleans defense held the Colts scoreless to make it 10–6 at the half. The Saints busted out of halftime by recovering a bold onside kick. Six plays later, QB Drew Brees hit RB Pierre Thomas with a pass behind the line of scrimmage at the Colts' 20, and Thomas twisted his way into the end zone to give underdog New Orleans its first lead.

Unflappable Colts QB Peyton Manning led the experienced Colts back—76 yards in ten plays, capped by Joseph Addai's own pinball-wizard run to put the Colts back on top, 17–13. A Saints FG made it 17–16 heading into the final 15 minutes. Then the Saints' defense stepped up, forcing the Colts into a long FG attempt that missed, and Brees stormed back. With 5:46 left, he hit TE Jeremy Shockey running a slant at the goal line, and a clutch two-point conversion put the Saints back up, 24–17.

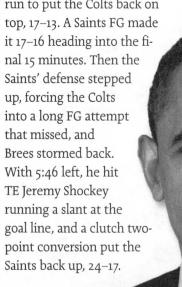

Still, the Colts had managed seven fourth-quarter comebacks during the season, and Manning can never be counted out. Another Colts' TD almost seemed inevitable, but then as Indy drove downfield it happened: Saints CB Tracy Porter stepped in front of Colts receiver Reggie Wayne, picked off a Manning pass, and took it to the house. Saints 31, Colts 17. A gigantic upset, a terrific game, and a storybook ending for the city of New Orleans.

Obama entered office amid the same kind of hopes many fans had for the Saints. He was the first African American president.

Already an historic figure when he took the oath of office, he promised more change. He had the smarts and the charisma, the popular mandate, and the congressional majority do get it done. Then he got smacked by reality.

A down economy led Obama to commit billions of dollars to a massive stimulus plan. He said he'd close the controversial prison at Guantanamo Bay, but couldn't work out the details. His attempts to reform healthcare were met by a tenacious "prevent" defense, intended to keep him from scoring many points. By the end of his first year—his first quarter—as Super Bowl XLIV kicked off, Obama had stopped the economy from spiraling into a depression, but it took a strident State of the Union speech and a feisty, televised discussion with Republican leaders to remind many people

why they'd voted for him. He began to show some muscle during 2010, his second quarter, pushing through a healthcare law that many opponents tried to block.

It's hard to compare Obama's presidency favorably to Super Bowl XLIV. After a sputtering start, the game just kept getting better. **The Super Bowls earn another point in the final match of America Bowl.** Outside of America Bowl, however, Obama still has time on the clock, and—as long as America keeps cheering for great football games and hoping for great presidents—he still has a chance to do the same.

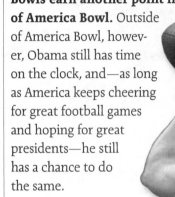

New Orleans Saints
QB Drew Brees

Super Bowl XLIV was a match between the best teams. The Saints were 13–0 before losing a game, and the Colts had reached 14–0.

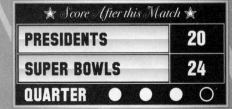

SUPER BOWL XLIV

SCORE: New Orleans Saints 31, Indianapolis Colts 17 **DATE:** February 7, 2010
LOCATION: Sun Life Stadium, Miami, FL
REGULAR SEASON RECORDS: Saints 13–3, Colts 14–2
GAME MVP: Saints QB Drew Brees **TV AUDIENCE:** 153, 4 million
COST OF 30-SECOND COMMERCIAL: $2.8 million

★ *Score After this Match* ★	
PRESIDENTS	20
SUPER BOWLS	24
QUARTER	● ● ● ○

APPENDIX

A wesome America Bowl Statistics and President/Super Bowl Fun Facts End Zone

ALL-TIME U.S. ELECTORAL VOTE LEADERS

Franklin D. Roosevelt	1876
Richard Nixon	1040
Ronald Reagan	1014
Dwight D. Eisenhower	899
Bill Clinton	749
Woodrow Wilson	712
Grover Cleveland	664
George H. W. Bush	557
William McKinley	563
George W. Bush	557
Herbert Hoover	503
Ulysses S. Grant	500
Andrew Jackson	496
Lyndon B. Johnson	486
Theodore Roosevelt	424
James Monroe	414
Warren G. Harding	404
Abraham Lincoln	392
Calvin Coolidge	382

MOST ALL-TIME ELECTORAL VOTES FOR A NON-PRESIDENT

William Jennings Bryan (ran 1896, 1900, 1908)	493
Thomas E. Dewey (1944, 1948)	288
Al Gore (2000)	266
Charles E. Hughes (1916)	254
John Kerry (2004)	251

PRESIDENTS WHO NEVER GOT ANY ELECTORAL VOTES

John Tyler

Andrew Johnson

Chester A. Arthur

PRO FOOTBALL HALL OF FAMERS WITH PRESIDENTS' LAST NAMES

Junois "Buck" Buchanan, DT, Kansas City Chiefs, 1963–1975

Bud Grant, coach, Minnesota Vikings, 1967–1983, 1985

Bob Hayes, WR, Dallas Cowboys, 1965–1974; San Francisco 49ers, 1975

Rickie Jackson, LB, New Orleans Saints, 1981–1993; San Francisco 49ers, 1994–1995

Jimmy Johnson, CB, San Francisco 49ers, 1961–1976

John Henry Johnson, RB, San Francisco 49ers, 1954–1956; Detroit Lions, 1957–1959; Pittsburgh Steelers, 1960–1965; Houston Oilers, 1966

Charley Taylor, WR, Washington Redskins, 1964–1975, 1977

Jim Taylor, RB, Green Bay Packers, 1958–1966; New Orleans Saints, 1967

Lawrence Taylor, LB, New York Giants, 1981–1993

Steve Van Buren, RB, Philadelphia Eagles, 1944–1951

Larry Wilson, S, St. Louis Cardinals, 1960–1972

Ralph Wilson Jr., owner, Buffalo Bills, 1960–

OTHER NOTEWORTHY NFL PLAYERS WITH PRESIDENTS' NAMES (FIRST OR LAST)

Gene Washington, WR, Minnesota Vikings, 1967–72; Denver Broncos, 1973 (played in Super Bowl IV)

Gene A. Washington, WR, San Francisco 49ers, 1969–1977; Detroit Lions, 1979

Mark Washington, DB, Dallas Cowboys, 1970–1978; New England Patriots, 1979 (played in Super Bowls X, XII, and XIII)

Roy Jefferson, WR, Pittsburgh Steelers, Baltimore Colts, Washington Redskins, 1965–1976 (played in Super Bowls V and VII)

Madison Monroe "Buzz" Nutter, LB, Baltimore Colts, 1954–1960, 1956; Pittsburgh Steelers, 1961–1964

Cleveland Jackson,* TE, New York Giants, 1979

Antonio Pierce, LB, Washington Redskins, 2001–2004; New York Giants, 2005–2009 (played in Super Bowl XLII)

Lincoln Kennedy,* OT, Atlanta Falcons, 1993–1995; Oakland Raiders, 1996–2003 (played in Super Bowl XXXVII)

Roosevelt Taylor,* DB, Chicago Bears, San Francisco 49ers, Washington Redskins, 1961–1972

James Harrison, LB, Pittsburgh Steelers, 2002– (played in Super Bowl XLIII)

Marvin Harrison, WR, Indianapolis Colts, 1996–2008 (played in Super Bowl XLI)

Rodney Harrison, DB, San Diego Chargers 1994–2002; New England Patriots, 2003–2006 (played in Super Bowls XXXVIII and XXXIX)

McKinley Boston, DE, New York Giants, 1968–1969

Roosevelt Grier, DT, New York Giants, 1955–1962; Los Angeles Rams, 1963–1966

Clinton Portis, RB, Denver Broncos, 2002–2003; Washington Redskins, 2004–

Reggie Bush, RB, New Orleans Saints, 2006– (played in Super Bowl XLIV)

These elite players have presidents' first and last names, joining actor Harrison Ford in an ultra-special club.

MOST SUPER BOWL GAMES BY A PLAYER

Mike Lodish, DT   6
(Super Bowls XXV, XXVI, XXVII, and XXVIII for Buffalo, and XXXII and XXXIII for Denver)

MOST WINNING SUPER BOWL GAMES BY A PLAYER

Charles Haley, LB/DE   5
(Super Bowls XXIII–XXIV for San Francisco, and XXVII, XXVIII, and XXX for Dallas)

MOST SUPER BOWL TOUCHDOWNS

Jerry Rice, 49ers (4 games)	8
Emmitt Smith, Cowboys (3 games)	5
Franco Harris, Pittsburgh (4 games)	4
Roger Craig, San Francisco (3 games)	4
Thurman Thomas, Buffalo (4 games)	4
John Elway, Denver (5 games)	4

MOST SUPER BOWL TEAM WINS

Pittsburgh Steelers	6
IX, X, XIII, XIV, XL, XLIII	
San Francisco 49ers	5
XVI, XIX, XXIII, XXIV, XXIX	
Dallas Cowboys	5
VI, XII, XXVII, XXVIII, XXX	
Oakland/L.A. Raiders	3
XI, XV, XVIII	
Washington Redskins	3
XVII, XXII, XXVI	

Green Bay Packers I, II, XXXI	3
New England Patriots XXXVI, XXXVIII, XXXIX	3
New York Giants XXI, XXV, XLII	3

MOST SUPER BOWL TEAM LOSSES

Minnesota Vikings IV, VIII, IX, XI	4
Denver Broncos XII, XXI, XXII, XXIV	4
Buffalo Bills XXV–XXVIII	4
Dallas Cowboys V, X, XIII	3
Miami Dolphins VI, XVII, XIX	3
New England Patriots XX, XXXI, XLII	3

SUPER BOWL PLAYERS WHO RAN FOR POLITICAL OFFICE

Lynn Swann (played in Super Bowl IX, X, XIII, and XIV for the Pittsburgh Steelers) ran for governor of Pennsylvania in 2006.

Jon Runyan (played in Super Bowl XXXIV for the Tennessee Titans and Super Bowl XXXIX for the Philadelphia Eagles) ran for U.S. Congress in New Jersey in 2010.

Peter Boulware (played in Super Bowl XXXV for the Baltimore Ravens) ran for a seat in the Florida House of Representatives in 2008.

PHOTO CREDITS